TRUE INT

BY

MK JUBB

CHAPTER ONE

Isabella tripped and fell flat on her face. She really wished she hadn't worn these stupid 4 inch heels now and gone for a more sensible shoe, after all it was only a job interview. Wearing heels probably wasn't the best idea she had had, but then again she rarely had a good idea, or so everyone kept telling her.

'Here Miss, let me help you up' Isabella looked up to see the buildings security guard leaning over with his hand held out.

'Oh, thank you. I'm such a clumsy cow' she took his hand and pulled herself up, brushing down her pencil skirt.

'Can you tell me where Mr Johnsons office is please, I'm here for an interview'. The guard pointed towards the lift.

'It's on the fifth floor. Turn right when you get out of the lift and it's the third door on the right'.

'Thank you' she smiled and hobbled over to the lift and pushed the button.

She reached the fifth floor and followed the corridor until she reached the right door. She knocked and entered when a brusque male voice bellowed "COME IN".

'SIT DOWN, I DON'T HAVE ALL DAY'.

'I'm here for the int....' He cut her off.

'YES, YES I KNOW VERY WELL WHY YOU'RE HERE. NOW GIVE ME YOUR C.V'. Why did he have to shout everything, couldn't the man talk like a normal person. Maybe he's not a normal person, maybe he's not even human. She tilted her head and squinted her eyes to try and get a better look at him. Did he have any horns, a tail perhaps? She tried to look around him, but couldn't see anything.

'MISS CRUZ, STOP DAYDREAMING. YOU HAVE'NT HEARD A WORD I HAVE SAID HAVE YOU? WELL SORRY BUT I WON'T BE EMPLOYING YOU TODAY. THANK YOU AND GOOD DAY. YOU CAN SEE YOURSELF OUT' and with that he got out of his chair and left the room.

Isabella sighed and shrugged her shoulders. Oh well just another job gone to the way side. She was used to it by now, so she didn't have any expectations when she went to interviews. Her friend Lorna had told her time and time again, if she looks and acts defeated she will never get a job.

As she turned the corner to where her flat was, she spied Lorna stood outside about to go in.

'LORNA' she called out to her friend and began to run, but her shoes wouldn't have any of that, and flat on her face she went again. Lorna turned and caught sight of her just as she was hitting the ground and cursed under her breath. She ran over to her and began to pull Isabella up off the floor.

'For fucks sake Izzy, what are you like. Girl you need to stop wearing those heels, one of these days you will break that

pretty neck of yours'. Izzy got to her feet and brushed herself
down. Twice in one day must be a record even for me, she
thought.

'I know Lorna, just please don't lecture me today, I'm not in
the mood' she leant down and removed her shoes. She
walked towards her building with Lorna in tow.

In her flat she threw her bag and shoes on the floor in the
entrance hall and went to the kitchen, grabbing a half
drunken bottle of white wine out of the fridge. She took two
glasses from the sink drainer and poured herself and Lorna
some wine.

'I need this after today. I don't get it. Why can't I get a job?
It's been three months now and nothing. What am I doing
wrong?' Lorna shrugged her shoulders at her friends
question.

'No, seriously Lorna, I need to know what it is about me that
employers see and won't give me a job'.

Lorna sighed deeply; she had told her friend many times
what the problem was. What else could she say, she never
listened anyway.

'Look Izzy, I have already told you what it is you do wrong so
it's up to you to change that. Anyway never mind that. The
reason I am here is I have a proposition for you, well kind of'.
Izzy sat up straight 'go on'.

'Well you know how my parents put an allowance in my bank
every month'. Izzy nodded. 'Well over the last few months I
haven't really needed anything so the money has

accumulated, so I was thinking, why don't you and I go do that backpacking thing we wanted to do after we finished Uni? I mean now is the perfect time. You don't have a job to go in to right away'.

Izzy shook her head 'that would be great if I had some money, but I don't have two pennies to rub together. I'm sorry but there is no way I could afford it'.

'Fuck Izzy, I could shake you sometimes. I will pay for the both of us. Come on, it will be fun. You have to come now anyway, because I've already booked our plane tickets'.

'WHAT! But i.. I can't, I mean how, I mean... I mean thanks' Izzy threw herself at Lorna and squeezed her tight.

'Izzy I can't breathe' she let go of her friend and spun around, giggling. She stopped spinning and turned to Lorna.

'Hang on a minute, where are we going?'

'NEW ZEALAND BABY'.

Izzy squealed and flung herself at her friend, AGAIN!

CHAPTER TWO

Feeling jet lagged, Izzy and Lorna strolled through the airport and outside to waiting taxi cabs. Izzy shaded her eyes as she took in her surroundings.

'Wow, Lorna this is amazing. I can't wait to get to the hotel and just chill out for the next 24hrs. Don't get me wrong, I'm looking forward to backpacking but relaxing by a pool first will be bliss'. Lorna nodded, agreeing with her friend.

'Right, let's get a taxi and get the party started Izzykins'. They jumped in a car and headed for their hotel of luxury before the real adventure started.

Their eyes widened in astonishment as they entered the hotel room. It was huge. Seemed more like an apartment, with its kitchen and living area. Three doors off to the left led to two large double bedrooms with adjoining bathrooms and a sauna. Talk about living like a queen. The girls squealed and ran in to each bedroom and flopping on the bed. Then running in to the other bedroom and doing the same.

'O.M.G, Lorna I can't believe this room. It's just so.... So ... oh fuck, you're the best friend ever doing all this. I don't know how I am ever going to repay you'. Lorna held up her hands and Izzy snapped her mouth shut.

'Babe, that big smile on your face is payment enough. You've had a pretty shitty year and this is me making you feel better, cos I loves ya don't I Izzykins. You're the bestest best mate I could have wished for'. Izzy did her usual flinging herself at her friend and knocked her on to the bed in the process. They giggled until they almost wet themselves, and then decided on a quick shower and change before heading out to sample the nightlife.

CHAPTER THREE

Izzy woke up with her head feeling the weight of a sledgehammer. She groaned as she tried to lift her head off the pillow. Hearing Lorna singing in the other room wasn't helping and she slumped her head down and covered it with the pillow to block out the noise.

Bang, bang on the door, and then Lorna came sweeping in with a tray. The smell of bacon and eggs emanated up Izzys nostrils. She moaned and squeezed the pillow tighter around her head.

'C'mon sleepy head, we have a long day of travelling ahead of us. I ordered room service, so get up, eat up and get showered'. Lorna announced, placing the tray on the bed and then leaving the room, slamming the door behind her, or so it sounded like to Izzy.

Izzy eventually surfaced from the bedroom, looking like she had been dug up. Lorna was sat on the sofa drinking a glass of orange juice and turned her head, following Izzy as she made her way towards the seat opposite and sat down.

'Jeez Izzy, you didn't half put it away last night! I think you drank the bar dry' Lorna laughed.

'I know, I know. How come you never get hangovers? I wish you could feel how I feel. I am never drinking again ....EVER'

Izzy said, reclining back on the sofa and snuggling in to the large cushion.

Lorna laughed at her friend 'like I haven't heard that before'. Izzy grabbed the cushion and threw it at her. Lorna ducked and the cushion caught a vase on the table behind her. They both watched in horror as it fell to the floor and smashed in to shards, scattering across the floor.

'Holy shit! Now look what you made me do' Izzy scalded.

'How was that my fault like?' Lorna asked.

'Well, you moved your head didn't you, so I missed your funny fat face'. Lorna gawped at her, then they fell about laughing.

'We had better get this mess cleaned up. So I'll do that while you go and get showered. It's 7.30am now and we need to get to the stop for 8.15 to get the bus. So hurry up Miss sloth'.

Izzy dragged herself up off the sofa 'ok slave driver. Don't worry I'll be quick' she said, when Lorna raised her eyebrow at her.

Twenty minutes later, Izzy was showered and dressed and heading towards the elevator door with Lorna.

'This is so exciting, our big adventure at last. Lorna if I forget to say it after we get back home, I want to tell you I had the best time ever'. Lorna smiled and gave her friend a big hug.

'Ditto, Izzykins'.

CHAPTER FOUR

The bus came to a grinding halt. The heat from the sun piercing through the windows on to Izzy cheek was becoming unbearable and she covered her face with her big floppy hat. 'I can't believe this heat. I thought the weather here was the same as in the Uk? And why have we stopped? We're in the middle of nowhere. Go and see what's happened Lorna'. Lorna sighed, exasperated at her friends laziness. Although she was feeling drained of energy from the heat herself, she dragged herself up and made her way to the front of the bus to find out why they had stopped.

Lorna made her way back to her seat and nudged Izzy, who had fallen asleep. Izzy grunted and lifted the floppy rim of her hat up to see her friend.

'So, the bus has broken down and we're waiting for another bus to come, which apparently won't be for another few hours. On the bright side though, someone is coming from the nearest store to deliver bottled water for everyone'. Izzy groaned at Lorna's declaration.

'Oh for fucks sake Lorna, I will survive another hour in this heat. Can't we just hitch a lift from here, you know like we were supposed to be doing anyway?'

'Look, we've come this far, why don't we wait until we get to the next town and then hitch from there? It would make more sense to do that. It is only going to get hotter as the day goes on and to be honest Izzy, I don't want to be walking in it'.

'Please Lorna, this heat is killing me. At least if we are walking we are still moving and getting somewhere, as opposed to being static like we are at the moment'.

Lorna sighed and looked at her friend. 'Ok, but only when they have been with the water. The last we want is to be dehydrated and collapsed at the side of a road'.

Izzy giggled and beamed at getting her own way. She was good at that at least.

At that moment a truck pulled up alongside the bus and two men jumped out. Grabbing cases of bottled water from the back, carried them on to the bus and began handing them out. Izzy had a thought. What if they asked these guys for a lift in to the net town? Then they wouldn't have to hitch on the road. She put the idea to Lorna.

'That way we can get to the next town before it gets dark' she ended, but Lorna wasn't too sure about this plan. Mostly because they had come from the opposite direction so would probably say no anyway.

'Oh, come on Lorna, we won't know until we ask. Well until you ask' Izzy said, with a cheesy grin.

'How come it's always me that has to ask all the time?'.

'Because, you're better at people skills than I am. Plus you're better at the flirting too'.

Lorna pursed her lips and got up. 'Fine, but next time there is any asking to do, it is your turn. GOT IT?'

Izzy shooed her friend away 'go on chick, you can do it'.

Lorna gave her friend an exasperated look and made her way down the bus and outside to the two men, who was now standing by their truck talking to the bus driver. They looked Lorna up and down as she approached.

'Hi guys, how are you doing?' she said, fluttering her eye lashes at them. They never said a word, just smiled at her.

'So anyway, my friend and i.....' she pointed to Izzy, whose face was now pressed against the window watching them.

'We were just wondering if you guys would be able to take us to the next town. Of course we would pay you for taking us'. The men looked at her blankly, then at each other before one of them finally spoke. 'Sure Miss'.

'Really? That's great, thanks. I'll tell my friend and get our bags'. Lorna rushed back on to the bus and told Izzy. They grabbed their bags and hurried over to the two waiting men, who were now sat inside the truck.

'Do we sit in the back of the truck?' asked Lorna.

'No, there is plenty of room for two little ones in here' one of the men said, patting the seat.

'Izzy, I'm not sure about this' Lorna whispered.

'It will be fine. Now get in' Izzy whispered back, digging her friend in the ribs.

They made themselves comfortable, best they could, considering they were cramped in like sardines in a tin. The driver, whose name was Bob, put the truck in to gear and set off. They were on their way. Next stop Taranaki.

CHAPTER FIVE

The truck came to a screeching halt. The girls almost going through the windscreen, if they hadn't have braced themselves.

'GET OUT MY TRUCK. NOW' the driver yelled at them.

The girls jumped out. They didn't need telling twice, they were just happy to be getting away from these creeps. Throughout the journey, the men had attempted to grope them. Izzy had knocked the guys hand away and told him not to touch her or she would call the police. He had laughed of course but then tried it on with Lorna, who told him, in no uncertain terms to "FUCK OFF". The men had called them prudes and frigid, hence why they had stopped the truck and telling them to get out.

The girls watched the truck drive away. Leaving a cloud of dust behind them. Looking around, they realised that they were in fact stranded in the middle of nowhere.

Izzy wiped sweat from her brow and plonked her floppy hat on her head. The sun was beating down on them like a spray of molten lava. Lorna check her backpack for the bottled water and found one.

'We're going to have to share' she said to Izzy. Shading her eyes from the sun, she saw a cluster of trees in the distance.

Perfect, she thought. At least they can be shaded until another truck or car comes along, or the bus for that matter. 'C'mon, there's some trees over there we can shelter under while we wait for a lift'. She grabbed Izzys hand, pulling her friend up, who was now sitting on the floor.

'Seriously, I cannot move with this heat. It's killing me'.

'Get a grip, it is not killing you. You are not dying. Now get up Izzy, otherwise I will leave you here and I'm not kidding' she informed her friend sternly.

'Fine, but if I drop down dead it's your fault'.

'Stop being so dramatic and get a move on. It's getting hotter as the hours pass and we need to get in to the shade'.

Izzy muttered something under her breath but it was too inaudible for Lorna to make out what she had said, so she let it pass. For now.

They reached the shaded area and sat down underneath one of the large trees.

'What now?' Izzy asked.

'We wait' Lorna said looking at her Izzys grumpy face 'look, I'm sure something will come along soon and we will be in the next town before we know it'.

The sun was starting to go down. They didn't know just how long they had been waiting but knew it had been hours. They had slept most of the afternoon under the large tree and now were getting agitated at not seeing any vehicles go passed. Izzy stood up to stretch her legs. Placing her hands on her hips, she bent backwards to stretch out her spine then

rotated her feet one at a time to loosen up her ankle joints.
Lorna was sat leaning against the trunk of the tree sipping at
the bottled water.

'Hey, save me some' Izzy hand gestured to her friend and
walked over to her.

'Sorry. Here' Lorna said and handed Izzy the bottle of water
that was now only a quarter full.

'What are we going to do if no-one passes? The water is
almost gone. Lorna I'm scared, what if....' Izzy took a deep
intake of breath, her eyes widened as she stared in to the
distance.

'Izzy what it is?' Lorna stood up and turned to see what Izzy
was looking at.

In the dusk light they could see what looked like two bright
piercing eyes glaring at them, surrounded by a dust cloud.
They appeared to be getting closer.

'Holy fuck. What is it?' Izzy whispered breathlessly 'It's
getting closer. Lorna what do we do?'

'I don't know'.

The girls clung together, terrified at what was approaching
them. Whatever it was, was making a low growling noise and
then screeched as it was almost upon them.

The girls cowered on the floor at the base of the tree.

CHAPTER SIX

They kept their eyes tightly shut as they held each other, wondering when this beast will attack. The anticipation was killing Lorna and she squinted her eyes open to get a look at the monstrous creature that was about to devour them.

A pair of brown boots, denim jeans, a large buckle belt. Her eyes raised upwards. Checked shirt….. this was no monster, it was a man stood before them and a gorgeous one at that. He stood at almost six feet tall with short scruffy looking dark brown hair, dark eyes that sparkled and that sexy stubble thing going on. Lorna could see from the tightness of his shirt that his body was toned too.

Lorna gulped and murmured 'wow'.

'Are you ladies ok? You know it's dangerous to be out here on your own?' the man said not as a question but as a statement.

Lorna almost swooned. Damn, that accent is so sexy.

Izzy looked up at this moment and gasped 'fucking hell it's Adonis'.

The man scowled down at them 'come, I'll take you somewhere that is safer than here'.

The girls looked at each other with more than a little concern on their faces. They had been in a predicament with those two men earlier. Did they really want to put themselves in that position again?

The man sighed when he realised the hesitation on their faces. 'Look, maybe we set off on the wrong foot. My name is Max, Max Veto and I have a farm a few miles from here. You're welcome to come and stay the night, and by that I mean I have spare rooms and plenty of space too. So it's up to you, I'll wait in the truck' and with that he turned on his heel and got back in his truck.

The girls just smiled at each other, as if they weren't going to go with him! They grabbed up their backpacks and ran to the truck, fighting to open the door because they both wanted to sit next to the delectable Max Veto. Lorna won.

'So Max where is this farm of yours? Is it a big one?' Lorna asked in a sultry tone. Max gave her a sideway glance and smiled as he noticed Izzy giving her friend a dig in the ribs.

'Ouch! What was that for' Lorna asked scornfully.

'Because you are acting like a tart. The man is letting us stay at his place for the night, the least we can do is be graceful and grateful'.

'Fine'.

They rode the rest of the journey in silence. Though Lorna did keep giving Izzy dirty looks. She was determined to get in to Max's pants and she didn't care if Izzy liked it or not. When it came to men Lorna was the queen and could just about get any man to sleep with her. She was beautiful to say the least; standing at five foot ten she was almost as tall as Max. Her long flowing blonde hair was shiny and glistened in the sun. She was slim with piercing blue eyes. Totally opposite to Izzy who wasn't a natural beauty. Izzy was five foot five with long dark brown hair, brown eyes and an hour glass figure (she claimed she was hippy, as in she had big hips) but her figure was the envy of some of her friends. She also had a small red love heart tattoo on her right ankle, an everlasting mistake from her teen years.

'WOW. Izzy look' Lorna gasped as they approached the entrance to the farm.
Izzy couldn't believe her eyes; it was like entering south fork from Dallas.
Max brought the truck to a halt at the top of a long gravel driveway.
'Ok girls grab your bags and I'll show you where you'll be sleeping' Max said as he slammed the truck door shut.
The girls didn't hesitate and quickly followed him as he made his way towards the large white wood door of the building that was to be their home for the night.

Their breaths were taken away by the large entrance hall. High ceilings, wood carved ornaments of horses on solid wood shelving units. A large circular table in the middle of the hall, upon which was the biggest vase of flowers the girls had ever seen in their life. The décor was tastefully done though with light oak furniture, natural coloured walls and natural wood flooring. The girls were in awe.

CHAPTER SEVEN

'Make yourselves at home. Supper is at seven thirty, I'm sure
you two must be starving, it's steak night tonight … hang on a
minute, you're not veggies are you? Cos I'm sure we can
rustle something up…' said Max.

'Oh no we eat meat and steak sounds great thanks …. And
thanks for letting us stay tonight, we appreciate it don't we
Lorna…… Lorna?' Izzy turned round to see Lorna sprawled
across the massive double bed they were to share.

'What? Oh yeh yeh thanks we appreciate it Max. You've been
very kind. Maybe I can repay you in some way' Lorna pushed
herself up on to her elbows and winked at Max. Izzy blushed
with embarrassment at her friends blatant attempts of
flirting with Max. She couldn't look Max in the eye but she
sensed he was watching her and not looking at Lorna. Why
did she feel so intimidated by him? She was no shrinking
violet herself but she had never openly flirted with any man,
she always knew if she clicked with someone and they would
become good friends before anything else ever happened.
Izzy was not and never has been a one night stand kind of
girl.

'That won't be necessary but thanks for the offer' Max
countered, still looking at Izzy. He was intrigued by her for

some reason. Max had had his fair share of women and Lorna was the type he would normally go for, but Izzy was something else. His cheek twitched as warmth emanated in his groin. For fucks sake what the hell was wrong with him. He didn't even know the girl and she was having a weird effect on him.

Izzy needed to break the tension in the room.

'By the way we haven't formally introduced ourselves. I'm Isabelle Cruz, but everyone calls me Izzy and this is my best friend Lorna Regan. You have a beautiful home and we're very grateful for your hospitality'.

Max smiled 'you're both welcome...oh just to warn you, my brother Mason will be dining with us tonight. He's the big city, suit wearing type and can be a little obnoxious, so please take whatever he says to you with a pinch of salt. He can be a .... What's the word I'm looking for ...oh yes, a knob head' he couldn't stop himself from laughing as the girls broke in to a giggle at his comment and description of his brother.

'Anyway girls, I have some work to finish off before supper, so I will see you later'.

The girls ogled his butt as walked away towards the spiralled staircase.

'HOLY FUCK' squealed Lorna 'Max is gorgeous; it was all I could do to keep my hands off of him. Hey what's up?'

'Nothing. Hey, maybe we should get showered and changed and go explore the house, after all he did say to make ourselves at home' Izzy tried to show and sound enthusiastic to try and change the subject. The last thing she wanted to do was try and explain what was wrong when she didn't even know herself. The only thing she did know was that Max made her feel weird, she just couldn't explain why or how. 'Cool, sounds like a plan. Me first' Lorna declared and ran in to the en-suite leaving Izzy stood there with her mouth gaping open. Typical Lorna, she thought and quietly chuckled to herself.

CHAPTER EIGHT

The girls ventured outside after nosing around the interior of the house and coming to the conclusion that this guy was minted.

'Look Izzy over there, stables. Let's go check out the horses, I've always wanted to ride but never had the opportunity'.

'Seriously Lorna, it's dark now and the last thing I want to do is step in horse poop, so I think I'll give it a miss'.

'Fine, do what you want, but I'm going to the stables. You can be such a spoil sport sometimes Izzykins.....see you at supper'.

Izzy watched her friend skip away. Suddenly she felt a cold shiver down her spine and sensed someone was standing behind her. She turned slowly.

'Well hi there missy, what do we have here then' the man drawled. His smarmy accent didn't match his dress sense. His dark grey suit and leather shoes didn't belong on a farm.

Izzy quickly realised that this guy must be who Max was talking about. His brother. His close proximity made her uncomfortable and she took a step back to distance herself only to stumble and almost fall on her arse. Luckily for her Max appeared out of nowhere and rescued her dignity.

'What the hell are you doing Mason? ..... are you ok Izzy?'

Max had wrapped his arms around her waist to hold her up and steady her before releasing his grip.

'Oh, yes, yes thank you' Izzy was grateful for his support but his touch made her feel flustered and it felt like an electricity volt had shot through her entire body.

Max couldn't explain what had just happened. What the hell was that he had just felt when he touched Izzy? Had she felt it too? …. Now wasn't the time, he had enough to worry about at the moment without a woman getting in the way.

'Mason I'll deal with you later, now go wash up for supper' demanded Max.

'But you haven't even introduced me properly yet'.

'Fine, Izzy this is my younger brother Mason Veto. Mason this is Izzy Cruz. Izzy and her best friend Lorna Regan are my guests for the night. Now why don't we all wash up for supper?'

Izzy shifted her feet, Mason made her feel uneasy. She didn't even know the guy but she knew she didn't like him. She would have to keep an eye on him and lock her bedroom door tonight; she didn't trust him as far as she could throw him.

It was at this point she remembered Lorna had gone to the stables.

'I need to get Lorna, she's at the stables. She went to look at the horses' Izzy burst out 'I'll go and get her real fast'. Izzy tried to compose herself as the men stared at her. A look of concern on Max's face and a look of lust on Masons.

'I won't be long' said Izzy and hurried along towards the stables. She called out to Lorna as she entered the stables and was met by a very dishevelled looking Lorna, followed by an equally dishevelled looking man. Izzy couldn't believe it. They had been here only a couple of hours and already her best friend had bedded a farm hand!

'Oh Izzy, I didn't see you there' Lorna had the audacity to blush when her sexy companion came up behind her and wrapped his arms around her waist and nuzzled her neck. The man winked at Izzy which only made her fidgety.

'Izzy this is Nick, he's Max's friend and works on the farm. We've been …. Errm …getting to know each other' Lorna giggled, squeezing Nicks hands.

'Yes well, Max as sent me to get you. It's time to wash up for supper. Will you be joining us Nick?'

Nick nodded 'yes, I live here on the farm; it's the little cottage just at the bottom of the lane. I eat supper every evening with Max. Do you know if his brother Mason is making an appearance tonight?' Nick had released his hold on Lorna and was now running fingers through his hair to try and tame the messed up locks.

'Yes, I just met him' Izzy admitted.

'Well by the look on your face you were not impressed. I don't blame you; personally I can't stand the man. He's a sleaze and I wouldn't trust him as far as I could throw him' declared Nick.

Her thoughts exactly, Izzy thought. She also knew that

instantly like this guy Nick, even he had just had his wicked way with her friend. She also knew that Lorna never did anything she didn't want to do, so knew her friend would have probably initiated it I the first place.

'Right, well as pleasant as it is standing here chewing the fat, I guess we better go and freshen up for supper. Bye for now Nicky boy, I'll see you at the dinner table, you have after all worked up an appetite' Lorna chuckled and skipped on in the direction of the house.

'Sorry about my friend, she can be a bit ... you know' said Izzy.

Nick laughed 'that's ok, I kind of like her. She gets under your skin pretty quickly'.

Izzy also laughed 'yes she does'.

CHAPTER NINE

Everyone ate their supper in silence. Stealing glances at each other. Izzy at Max and vice versa when they thought each weren't looking, but caught one another a couple of times and secretly smiled to themselves. Lorna on the other hand was very blatant at her flirtation with Nick and him with her. They were pretty obvious to everyone witnessing, that they had mutual sexual attraction between them.

Max broke the ice.

'Would anyone like a top up?' he said, holding up a bottle of red wine.

'Not for me Max, I need something a little stronger. Would anyone care for a brandy?' asked Mason.

'No not for me thank you' said Izzy.

'I second that' Lorna concurred 'actually I think I'm ready for bed. How about you Nick, are you ready for bed?' Lorna hadn't taken her eyes off of Nick all through supper. Izzy could see she was smitten and who could blame her. He was a good looking guy with his toned tanned skin, blonde tousled hair and brown eyes. Izzy had also noticed in the stables that he had a tattoo sleeve, a beautiful Maori tattoo at that and he was about as tall as Max too. No wonder Lorna fancied him.

Izzy looked over at Mason. His smarmy smirk made her feel sick. The way he was looking at Lorna and Nick in a provocative way made her uncomfortable. She shifted in her seat. Maybe another glass of wine will take the edge off.

'I wouldn't mind another glass of wine Max, please' she gave Max her best wide gleaming smile.

He got up off his seat and walked around the table to where she sat holding up her glass ready for a refill.

'Thank you Max'.

'You are very welcome Izzy'.

They held each other's gaze for what seemed like an age. Her heart pounding so fast it felt like it would jumped out of her chest and his breathing deepened as he became overwhelmed by the look of passion in her eyes.

'Well this is all entertaining and such, but I have an important meeting in the morning so I won't be staying overnight, if it's all the same to you brother dear' Mason declared.

Max never moved his gaze from Izzy and swept is hand in dismissal of his younger brother. He had little time for him, but he helped with the financial side of running the farm. He was good at that at least. Their parents had both been killed in car accident five years ago, their will stated that both sons got 50/50 stake in the farm. It also stipulated that for the eldest son to gain full control of the farm (meaning Max) then he would have to marry before his 35th birthday. Max hadn't been interested in this part of the will though, he was happy to share with Mason. But Max had been having second thoughts about it lately. His brother had been acting weird the last couple of years and he couldn't figure out why. He knew it wasn't anything to do with a woman in Masons life, because Mason didn't do relationships. Yes he had had women but it was mostly paid services, this much Max knew. Max hadn't actively been looking for someone to be his wife. Hell, he only had to snap his fingers and at least five women would come running, he knew this because these women had made it pretty damn clear they were up for being Mrs Max Veto. Yes, time was running out, he would be 35 in three months time but Max was an old fashioned guy and would only marry the woman he loved and if it didn't happen then it didn't happen. He wasn't going to cry over it.

When he eventually looked round, Mason, Lorna and Nick had all left leaving him alone with Izzy.

Well this could get interesting, he thought.

'Would you like to take the wine and sit on the porch Izzy?'

Izzy nodded. Was he stupid? Of course she wanted to be with him. She gagged her mouth with her hand. Did she just say that out loud? Or are her thoughts just really loud.

Max gave her a quizzical look 'are you ok Izzy?'

'What? Oh yes sorry, I was just thinking. Sorry. Yes I would love to come and sit on the porch'.

The sky was clear. You could see the constellation shining bright in its infinite galaxy. There was a soft cool breeze in the air that took away the edge off the humid heat.

They sat quietly, just taking in the breath taking view of the night sky. It's amazing, Izzy thought. She had never even thought to sit outside in the evening at home in England and just look up at the stars. Then again the sky was cloudy most of the time so you couldn't see the stars any way.

'It's beautiful' she whispered, almost to herself.

'I think so too'.

Izzy looked round at Max to see him looking at her.

'Oh' was all she could say. Max leaned over and gently kissed her on the cheek.

'Maybe it's time we went to bed' Max said and then noticed the panic on Izzy's face. 'No, sorry I meant I go to my bed and you go to yours, to sleep. I never meant for you to get the wrong idea. Maybe I shouldn't have kissed you but I couldn't help myself. I really don't know what is happening to me at the moment. Since you crashed in to my life I haven't been able to think of anything or anyone else. What have you done to me Isabella Cruz?'

What could she say to that? She didn't know what to say. But she had to say something because staring at him open mouthed, looking like a wally wasn't cutting it.

'Errm ... oh ... right .... Ok ... yes ...' she stuttered. If she hadn't felt dumb before, she certainly did now.

'BED..... YES TIME FOR BED' she spluttered a little too loudly. She jumped up and without another word practically ran through the house, up the stairs and in to her bedroom, locking the door for good measure. She slapped her palm on her forehead. 'Dumb...dumb....dumb that's what I am' she muttered to herself. How will she be able to face him in the morning now? She behaved like an utter twonk and he's going to hate her and kick them out. What am I talking about? She needed Lorna; at least she will talk some sense in to her. She scanned the room but there was no sign of her friend. Great! She knew exactly where she was, with Nick at his cottage. Fanfuckingtastic! She had no option but to get ready for bed and at least try to get some sleep.

CHAPTER TEN

Izzy tentatively made her way down the stairs and towards the kitchen. She needed strong black coffee and maybe a reality check after last night's debacle. Embarrassed was an understatement. She couldn't believe he had kissed her in the first place because she hadn't expected it, but to then assume all he wanted to do was to have sex with her! Well that was the topping on the cake.

She wondered what would happen now. Would he throw them out? Act like nothing had happened? Or worse, want to talk about it?

Izzy squirmed at the idea. She didn't want to talk about it, she just wanted to forget what had happened and hopefully he will let them stay. She loved his farm and as much as she wanted to see the rest of New Zealand, she had to admit to herself that she liked Max and didn't want to leave.

As she pushed through the kitchen door, Max was stood leaning against the sink drinking a cup of hot steaming coffee, he was wearing grey pyjama bottoms that hung on his hips, showing his abs and the trail of hair going down to his groin. He was looking down intently at the cup. Izzy studied him for a second then got all flustered when he looked up at her and smiled. She stumbled in to the door frame.

'Hey, be careful' Max said, rushing over to steady her. With coffee cup in one hand and one hand on her waist, he managed to make it look like he was saving her from a dangerous incident. Even if it was only a door frame, he made her feel safe, which of course was just ridiculous, because they had only just met, but that is how he made her feel.

'Thanks. I'm such a plonker sometimes' Izzy said, scraping her hair back and tying it back with bobble she had around her wrist.

'Plonker? What does that word mean?' Max asked.

Izzy laughed, how could he not know what a plonker is. She then remembered where she was. New Zealand. They obviously hadn't heard of that expression here. Max also looked cute with the puzzled expression on his face.

'Oh right yeh' she muttered under her breath 'well a plonker is someone who does silly things' she said a little bit louder then quickly said 'but not on purpose though, by accident. Like me. I'm a 100 carat plonker' she nervously giggled. She then realised that Max still had his hand on her waist and was pulling her in to him.

He lightly brushed his lips against her temple. She was sure he also sniffed her hair at the same time. She didn't care though because the scent of him made her weak at the knees. For fucks sake, what was this man doing to her.

He pulled away abruptly and walked over to the sink, placing his cup in the soapy water. He cursed under his breath. She was driving him insane. He hardly slept a wink last night because all he could think about was Izzy. Her soft milky skin and how he wanted so much to touch it, stroke it and kiss it. He wanted to see her naked, to make love to her, to pleasure her. At this moment all he knew was that he didn't want her to leave today, but how could he make her stay? He had no right to ask her, no right to force her. He racked his brain for something, an idea but nothing was popping I to his head. DAMN IT! He screamed in his head.

'What time are you thinking of leaving?' He gripped the edge of the sink. Hoping, wishing that she would say she wanted to stay.

'I'm not sure' she said, almost a whisper. She inwardly groaned. He must be embarrassed and can't wait to get rid of them.

'I guess I had better get dressed and fill the truck. I'll drop you off at the next town, you should be able to pick up the bus from there no problem' he stared at her intently for a second then walked towards her. She side stepped to let him pass.

'Thanks. Izzy I …..'

'Yes?'

'Please help yourself to some breakfast and i hope you enjoy the rest of your trip'.

Izzy sighed. I guess that is that. Well it was fun while it lasted, she thought.

CHAPTER ELEVEN

Izzy plonked her holdall on the floor next to the front door and checked her watch. It was lunch time and still no sign of Lorna. She had wanted to go down to the cottage to drag her friend out so they could get the hell out of there, but after Max had left the kitchen that morning, she had a quick slice of toast then rushed back to her room, locking the door. She had taken her time to get ready and waited until she knew Max had left the house. She had watched from behind the curtain, Max leaving the house and walking towards the stables before she risked venturing out of her room. She knew she was acting like an idiot, but facing him again was just too much for her bear. The effect he had on her was driving her crazy and she had to snap out of it because after today she was never going to see him again.

She checked her watch again and cursed under her breath. What was taking her friend so long? Stamping her foot she picked up her holdall and swung open the front door. She gasped when she saw Mason stood there.

'Hello Izzy. Sorry I didn't mean to scare you'.

She hated the drawl in his tone. His smarminess creeped her out.

'Oh you didn't, I was expecting to see you stood there that's all. If you're looking for Max he's in the stables. Please excuse me, I have to go and get Lorna'. She tried to slide passed him but he put his hand across the door frame, blocking her path. 'What, you're leaving so soon? I was hoping we could get to know each other better' he lifted his hand to stroke her cheek but she flinched away. Mason took a step forward and grabbed her hair, pulling her head back. Izzy struggled to break free and tried to pound on his chest with her fist but he was too strong.

'No-one rejects me' he said through gritted teeth before kissing her hard.

Shock emanated through her body as she looked down to Mason sitting on the floor rubbing his chin. She had spaced out for a second and hadn't realised or heard Max come in, grab Mason off of her and punch him.

'WHAT THE FUCK DO YOU THINK YOU'RE DOING' Max shouted at his brother.

'TOUCH HER AGAIN AND I'LL KILL YOU, DO YOU HEAR ME? NOW GET YOUR ASS OUT OF MY HOUSE'.

Izzy looked from one brother to the other. She felt like she had to do something but didn't know what. Her instinct was telling her to go to Max and comfort him, so that's what she did. She placed her arm around his and laid her head on his shoulder. Max automatically put his arm around her waist and looked down at her, deep in to her eyes. That look was telling her she was safe with him. He gave her a reassuring squeeze.

Mason dragged himself up off the floor and straightened his tie.

'That is a big mistake brother dear and you will pay for hitting me'.

'Bring it on Mason because I have had enough of the way you treat women. You see them as objects to use and abuse for your pleasure. Well that aint going to happen to Izzy, she is off limits...'

Izzy whispered Lorna's name.

'....and that goes for her friend Lorna too. Touch either one and you will wish you had never been born'.

Mason picked his briefcase off the floor and headed out the door before stopping and turning back to them.

'Oh by the way Max, the reason I was here in the first place was to remind you that you only have sixty days left. I sure hope you fail then I will finally get what I deserve. Goodbye Izzy, enjoy your time travelling in New Zealand' he turned on his heel and left.

'What did he mean?' Izzy asked.

'It's nothing for you to worry about. Come on I'll make you coffee and I'll give Nick a call and tell him to bring Lorna back'.

Izzy smiled up at him and Max couldn't resist, he leaned in for a kiss then stopped.

'Sorry' he said. But Izzy wasn't accepting that, she wanted him to kiss her. She wrapped her hands round his neck and pulled him to her. The kiss was light and soft. But the heat that ran through both of them was extreme and the kiss became more passionate. She felt him harden against her abdomen. He trailed kisses across her cheek and down her neck.

'What are you doing to me?' he whispered against her soft skin.

'HONEY I'M HOME…. OOPS SORRY' Lorna's bellowing voice broke in to the moment and they pulled apart quickly.

'Well this is awkward' Lorna said, and then noticed the holdall by the door.

'Change of plan Izzykins, well that if it is ok with lover boy here……' she giggled 'we're staying here for a bit. We have plenty of time to explore the rest of New Zealand. Nick says he would love to show us the sights of the local area, that there is plenty to do here so I thought, why not'.

Izzy looked at her friend with disbelief. Lorna just smiled and looked from Izzy to Max with an expectant look on her face waiting for his answer.

For Max it was a no brainer, of course his answer was yes. He wanted Izzy to stay, he wanted Izzy period! He was pretty sure she felt the same way, but he didn't want to push it. He had to play it cool.

'Well it's entirely up to you. I mean you're both welcome to stay for as long as you want. As you have seen there is plenty of space and as Nick as said there's plenty to do. I could teach you to ride if you like' he looked down at Izzy when he said the last bit.

It was Lorna who spoke for both of them 'I guess we're staying then' she rushed over to Izzy and hugged her. Wow, this was a turnaround; it was usually Izzy who got all giddy and hugged Lorna to almost death!

'Suppose I had better go take my bag back upstairs' Izzy stated as she watched her friend run up the stairs.

'Please let me' Max leaned down and grabbed up the holdall.

'Thank you Max' the butterflies in her stomach felt like they were about to burst out at any moment. She couldn't believe her luck. Thanks Lorna, I knew there was a reason why you're my best friend, she thought.

CHAPTER TWELVE

For the last four days Izzy and Lorna had be shown some of
the delights of the local area. Max and Nick had taken them
out for meals and they had tasted some of the local
delicacies. Max had talked Izzy in to letting him teach her to
ride and this morning was to be her first lesson. She hadn't
even been to look at horses in a field back home let alone be
up close and personal. She was bricking it to say the least.
She looked at herself in the mirror, the riding attire that Max
had provided fitted her perfectly and she wondered who
they had belonged to. His ex –wife or girlfriend maybe? She
didn't know how she felt about that but didn't like to ask.
She brushed herself down and turned to leave the bedroom.
She was about to grab for the bedroom door handle when
someone knocked on the door. She opened it to see Max
stood there in all his riding gear glory. Fuck, why did he have
to look so damn sexy in everything he wears?
She really couldn't stand to be near him sometimes, because
she wanted to touch him, to kiss him and for him to do the
same to her. But other than the day she was supposed to be
leaving, he hadn't made anymore advances, but then neither
had she. They had pretty much reverted to been "friends"
and anything else felt like it was out of bounds. She yearned

for his hands to caress her body. She closed her eyes, imaging their naked bodies entwined.

'Izzy, are you ok?'

She suddenly snapped out of her daydream when she heard Max.

'What? Oh yes, yes I'm ok. Sorry. I'm ready to go if you are' she was flustered and she knew that he knew it. She blushed as he stepped aside allowing her to pass.

He looked solemn this morning; she thought and wondered what was making him feel that way. After what his brother Mason had said the other day, she hadn't been able to get it out of her head. What had he meant about Max only having sixty days left? Max had acted like it was nothing but his mood since had been pretty down. He looked like he had the weight of the world on his shoulders and she didn't like seeing him like this, like he was pained or something.

Izzy sneaked a couple of glances at Max as they walked towards the stables in silence. Little did she realise that he had done the same to her. The silence was killing them both, but neither one could think of anything appropriate to say to the other. He wanted to tell her that as crazy as it seemed he was falling for her, but with his life been complicated at the moment and with this deadline he was dealing with, the last thing he wanted was for her to think he wasn't sincere about his feelings. He had to box clever so he can get everything he wants.

Izzy always thought it was bonkers to fall in love with

someone at first sight. She used to laugh at people who said such a silly thing that is until now, now that she was experiencing it herself. Now she understood.

As they turned in to the stables, Nick was just leading one of the already saddled horses out. Something must have spooked the horse because it reared up on to its hind legs and kicked out its front one, catching Izzy and knocking her to the ground. Nick tried with all his might to control the beast. Max swore and grabbed at the reigns. Between them they managed to get the horse back in to the stable and bolt the door. Max rushed over to Izzy.

'Izzy are you alright? Please speak to me, say something' Max was panicking. Izzy was laid out, her eyes closed. Max stroked her hair back off of her face.

'Izzy wake up, please my darling wake up'.

She slowly opened her eyes. They were a little blurred but she could tell it was Max looking down at her. She tried to sit up.

'No wait' Max said. He wrapped her arms around his neck then lifted her up.

Nick stepped forward. 'Izzy I'm so sorry. He's usually pretty placid, fuck knows what spooked him like that but I will find out for sure'.

Izzy couldn't speak, she just nodded.

'I'll just make her comfortable then I'll come back and get to the bottom of this' Max said before giving a curt nod to Nick and walking off carrying Izzy back towards the house.

He took her in to the living room and laid her on the sofa. He left the room and came back with a glass of water.

'Here sip this. Are you hurt anywhere?' he asked while feeling down her arms then her legs for any broken bones. She shook her head 'no I'm not hurt, just a little shaken. See this is why I don't go near horses'.

'You're scared of horses? Why didn't you tell me instead of letting me talk you in to it?' he scraped fingers through his hair and cursed under his breath.

'I'm sorry. It's not your fault. I don't understand what could have spooked Benson. He's one of the gentler horses, that's why I had him saddled up for you. You rest here for now, I need to go check something. I won't be long'.

Izzy grabbed his arm as he went to get up.

She needed him, she wanted him. She pulled him close to her. Their lips almost touching, their breath hot with desire as their eyes burned in to each other's souls.

He wanted to kiss her so bad but couldn't bring himself to do it. The last thing he wanted to do was take advantage of her. He pulled away from her and stood up. 'I'm sorry Izzy, I can't give you what you want. I so wish I could but my life is so complicated right now and I don't want you to be in the middle of it. I don't want you to get hurt'.

Izzy swung her legs round and stood up next to him.

'I don't care Max. I'm sick of having these feeling for you and not been able to show you or do anything about it. You maybe can't admit it but I won't hold it in any longer. God knows how long we will be here at the farm for or when we will be going back to England but right now I want to be here with you. I want you and I want you to kiss me and make love to me until I can't walk, until I can't breathe'. She took hold of his hand and lifted it to her mouth, pressing her lips to the palm of his hand.

'It's too quick Izzy. You don't know how you feel, not really. I'm not sure even I know what it is I am feeling. There is something there I know that much but now is not the right time...' he tucked a loose strand of hair behind her ear '..... I have to go and help Nick. I promise you we will talk properly when it's the right time'.

Izzy nodded, what more could she say or do. He was asking her to wait and god damn it he was worth waiting for.

She watched him walk away. Her heart felt heavy. She had fallen in love with this beautiful stranger. Cupid had well and truly pierced her heart with his arrow.

CHAPTER THIRTEEN

Nick was in the paddock with Benson by the time Max returned. He had something in his hand studying it when Max approached him.

'What's that?' he asked Nick.

'Some sort of dart. Look' he handed it to Max.

Max looked intently at it. He had seen something like this before on his travels to Africa many years ago. He also knew that his brother Mason had been there and had brought a blow pipe back as a souvenir. The bastard, it had to be him. The thought that Izzy could have been badly injured or killed because of his brother made him feel sick to the stomach.

'Max, I know what you're thinking. I know he's got one but do you seriously think he would do something like this? I know he can be a bit…. Well you know… but really ..' Max shushed him.

'Put Benson away then come to my office' Max said before storming off towards the house.

Nick knew this wasn't going to be pretty. The brothers had always fought but this was on another level. Knowing Max like he did, he knew his friend would not let this go and Mason was going to get it with both barrels.

Nick knocked on the door to Max's office and entered without been prompted. Max said bye to whoever he had been talking on the phone with and replaced the receiver. 'Take a seat Nick' Max said as he walked around his desk and sat on the edge facing Nick.

'Ok Max, what's the plan?'

'Remember me telling you about the conditions of my parents will? Well my fathers to be specific'.

'Errr yes... do you think that's what all this is about? Mason trying to scupper everything?' Nick asked, not comfortable now with sitting, he got up and paced back and forth 'holy shit, I know the dude is your brother Max but that shit is just messed up'.

'I concur. The thing is.......well it's Izzy'.

Nick whistled and stopped pacing 'Dude she is hot. Have you and her you know' he winked at Max.

'What! No nothing like that.....but i....' Max couldn't get the words out. As much as Nick was his best friend they had never spoken or opened up to each other about their feelings, it was just too wussy. But Max needed to tell someone how he felt and Nick was his only option. Normally he would have talked to his mother. He so missed her and the long walks they took together, talking about everything and anything, putting the world to rights.

'Bro, you've fallen for her haven't you? Wow man, that's great. So what is the issue?' Nick asked.

'The issue is we have only just met. How can I tell a girl I just met that I am in love with her, when I'm not quite sure myself if that is what I actually feel. Maybe it's just lust, I am in lust with her. Just doesn't quite have the same ring to it really' Max walked back around his desk and deflated in to his chair.

'Look, I know what you're trying to say bro, but you can't let this stop you. Whatever Mason is up to, you can't let him win. If you feel anything for this girl you have to tell her. I mean you have loads of time to make it work so what's the problem?' Nick said as he sat back down in the chair.

'The problem is I have just over fifty days left and I have no clue what to do. The last thing I want is for Izzy to think I am using her, so do you understand now why I can't say anything to her?'

Nick scraped his finger through his hair, to say he was shocked by the revelation was an understatement. His mate was in a bind and he couldn't think of any way whatsoever to help his best friend.

'Fuck Max. I don't know what to say. Your dad really fucked you over didn't he?' Which was more of a statement than a question.

'That my friend is an understatement.......i just need to put a plan in to place to stop Mason from getting everything. I don't know how yet but I have to think of something soon or I will lose everything my parents worked hard for and I'm damned if I am going to let that happen'.

CHAPTER FOURTEEN

Izzy stretched out and yawned. She had slept like a log last night. The two bottles of red wine she had downed with Lorna was probably the reason why. They had locked themselves away in their room, drank, talked about Max and Nick and giggled most of the night before slumber took hold of them both.

She looked over at her friend who was laid out on the floor, dribbling on to the cushion she had dragged off of the small two seater sofa situated at the foot of the bed.

Izzy chuckled at the sight of Lorna and then groaned when she remembered what she had told her about her feelings for Max. Lorna knew how easily Izzy could fall for a guy and would always caution her! But last night Lorna had told her to go for it. She had been drinking though so she decided to brush the advice aside and for once listen to what Lorna would normally say "don't rush in where fools fear to tread". Izzy never understood the saying but she was sure it meant for her not to give her heart to anyone so easily.

She rolled over and checked the time on her phone, 11.30am. Crap! They had missed breakfast. She then realised that she was pretty ravenous. Her tummy rumbled.

She crept out of bed as quietly as possible so as not to

disturb Lorna and tip toed to the en-suite. She took a quick shower and dressed before venturing back in to the bedroom.

Lorna was sat on the edge of the bed, looking a little worse for wear.

'Why didn't you wake me Izzykins? Why are you dressed? What time is it?'

'It's almost twelve and I'm dressed because my tummy won't stop rumbling. Are you coming down for something to eat?' Lorna fell back on the bed and groaned.

'I'll take that as a no then shall i?' Izzy picked a cushion off the floor and threw it at Lorna.

'Hey' said Lorna and threw it back.

'That's my cue to leave' Izzy said, rubbing her tummy as it rumbled again.

'I'll CATCH YOU IN A BIT' Lorna called out to Izzy as she exited through the door.

Izzy sneaked down the stairs and through the house towards the kitchen. After yesterday's debacle she didn't want to run in to Max, at least not right now. Her tummy sounded like a volcano erupting the noise it was making. She slowly pushed the kitchen door open and scoped the room, it was clear. She sighed and made her way to the large double doored fridge. Sticking her head inside she perused to see what she could make to eat. Something quick, she thought. Too engrossed with what was in the fridge, she hadn't heard anyone enter the kitchen.

She grabbed some eggs, a red pepper and the block of cheese and stood up to close the door.

'ARRGHH!' She screamed out, dropping the arm full of food on the floor.

'Shit, Izzy I'm sorry. I didn't mean to scare you' Max reached out to her but Izzy stepped back and leaned against the sink, trying to catch her breath.

'Izzy, are you ok? Please, here take a seat' Max pulled out a dining chair and gestured for her to sit.

Izzy pushed away from the sink and staggered towards the chair. Max cursed under his breath.

'Fuck, I really scared you didn't i? I'm sorry, the last thing I want to do is scare you. I want to…. I mean…. Sorry I'm not good at this, I'm out of practice. Sorry'.

She sat down and let out a deep sigh 'Max, I wish you would just say what it is you want to say to me. I think I already know, but I want to actually hear you say it, because I am going around the bend not knowing for sure. I keep thinking maybe I am imagining it or……' before she had chance to finish speaking Max had bent down and was kissing her full on the lips. He cupped her face and kissed the tip of her nose before pulling out another chair and sitting facing her.

'You're not imagining it Izzy. I have these feelings that I can't explain, because one, I am not very good at talking about my feelings and two, it's a lot more complicated and the latter I can't explain for a number of reasons. But believe me when I say I feel the same way as you do. I just can't do anything right now. I'm sorry Izzy, It's probably not what you want to hear but this is all I can do at the moment'.

Izzy sat silent until he had finished talking, then mulled over what he had said.

'Explain to me what "this" is' she asked.

'I don't know. What I do know is that I don't want you to leave. I like you been around. It's been really nice having company. Other than Nick it's just me rattling around this big house. Please stay. I want you to stay'.

Izzy searched his face and saw the pleading in his eyes. How could she be sure he wanted her to stay because he had feelings for her or because he was just lonely? What she did know was she wanted to stay. Hell, she would stay forever if he asked her to. Her tummy rumbled. Max laughed.

'Let me make you something eat. I missed you at breakfast. Assume you and Lorna had a good evening'.

He was changing the subject. He knew it and he knew she knew it too. He busied himself cleaning up the mess on the floor then proceeded to make Izzy some scrambled eggs.

'Thanks Max' she said.

CHAPTER FIFTEEN

Lorna had been spending a lot of time with Nick at his cottage in-between his farm chores. Izzy was fine with that because it meant her and Max spent time together. He was always tactile with her, it was as if he had to have some body contact with her. He would touch her arm, place his hand on her waist, scrape a loose strand of hair from her eyes, anything was an excuse for him to touch her. What she really craved was him inside of her, something she hoped would happen at some point.

Max had taken her down to the, what he called the family lake. He told her about when he and Mason were boys, how they played and swam in the lake, the canoeing and the picnics his mum would prepare for the four of them with enough food to feed an army. Izzy saw the pain and the love in his eyes as he talked about his parents. She could tell they used to be a close family and wondered what had happened, why Mason was the way he was.

They lay side by side on a blanket by the lake, their fingers slightly touching. Having tucked in to a lovely picnic they were letting their tummy settle. Max had suggested a swim in the lake and though Izzy reminded him twice that she hadn't brought her swimsuit, Max had just smiled and winked. He rolled on to his side, looking down at her. Izzy shaded her eyes from the sun with her hand.

'What?' she asked.

'Are you ready for that swim yet? Because I am. Come on' he stood up and held out his. Izzy giggled.

'I told you, I haven't brought my .....'

'Swimsuit. Yeah yeah, I know. But neither have I ....' He scanned around '.......there is no-one to see us. The coast is clear'.

'Do you mean skinny dipping?'

The look of shock on her face was a picture and made him laugh.

'Not exactly, I was thinking more like in your underwear but if you want to skinny dip, I'm game if you are' he laughed again.

'Fine, I guess underwear is like a swimsuit. How deep is it? There's no like big fish or anything that could bite me in there?' she looked at him with a side glance.

'No I promise you, there is nothing in there can bite you and it's as deep as I am tall, so your feet should pretty much touch the bottom. So are we good to go?' he took a hold of her hand and stroked it with his thumb.

'Ok, but turn around while I get undressed and get in the water' she twiddled her finger at him to turn around.

He turned his back on her and waited. When he heard a splash he turned back round to see her neck deep in the water. He started to undress himself then stopped and called out to her. 'Hey, what's good for the goose is good for the gander. Look the other way until I get in'.

Izzy tutted and faced the other way. She hadn't heard him get in to the water. She was startled when he came up behind her and wrapped his arms around her waist.

'Oh' was all she could say. He pulled her close to him, a little too close because she could feel his hardness. She wondered if he knew, then shook her head at the stupidity of her thought. Of course he knew and the glint in his eye also told her that he knew she knew!

'Let's go for a swim. Do you see that small island over there? Do you think you can make?' he asked.

Izzy nodded and watched him swim away. She tried to keep up but he was more athletic than her and made it to the island pretty quickly. He pulled himself up and dangled his feet in the water waiting for her.

She was a good swimmer, very graceful, he thought. As she approached he stood up and leaned down to grab her hand to help her up.

Izzy couldn't take her eyes off him. She had watched him lift himself up on to the island. The rippling muscles in his arms and when he had turned around and shook the excess water from his hair, he looked like Adonis. His taut abs was turning her to jelly and she wasn't sure she would make it to the island, it was sheer adrenaline that actually got her there. As he helped her up he pulled her close, he couldn't resist any longer, and the heat in his groin was unbearable. He didn't want to force her or make her feel uncomfortable but the swim across to the island in the cold water hadn't worked to stem his desire for her.

Izzy could not only sense his desire but feel it against her body. Oh god, was he finally going to seduce her. She looked around to check no-one was around. Looking deep in to one another's eyes she run her hands over his body, moving them down, slightly brushing over his hard cock. Max gasped, he hadn't been touched like this in a long time. He grabbed her hand and brought it to his mouth, kissing it.

'Izzy are you sure' he whispered.

'Yes. Please don't make me wait any longer, I don't think I could stand it'.

He cupped her face and kissed her hard. He lowered her down on to the ground, parting her legs as laid on top of her. His right hand stroked and caressed her body as he moved his mouth from her lips down her neck, her decollate. He kissed between her breasts. She undid her bra and he lifted his head for a second while she removed it. He slowly lowered his head and took a nipple in to his mouth.

Izzy arched her back as her whole body tingled under the sensation. Her fingers grabbed at his hair, entwining it between them.

Max left her nipple and kissed her again, rubbing himself against her pubis.

Izzy couldn't stand it any longer and reached down to remove her panties. Max moved his hand down too and helped her remove them before grappling with his own wet boxers and removing them. He positioned himself back on top, easing in to her damp pussy. Izzy groaned as the pleasure emanated throughout her body.

Max started slow. Kissing her with every thrust. He wasn't sure how long he could hold out for, he felt like he was on the verge but he didn't care, this felt good and he could always pleasure her afterwards. Hell at this rate he would probably get hard again anyway. Izzy was hot and she made him hot.

Izzy groaned. Her breathing getting heavier as Max thrust harder and faster. She wrapped her legs around him, clinging to him, feeling his sweat drip on her brow as they both climaxed together.

He slumped down on her shoulder, his breathing fast and heavy. Their skin clammy as they held each other. What just happened had been so intense and they needed to catch their breath before either one could move. They lay for what seemed like an age when Max eventually rolled off on to his back. They lay silent looking up at the clear blue sky. They didn't need to speak because they had just said everything with actions rather than words.

CHAPTER SIXTEEN

Mason knocked on Max's office door. When there was no answer he invited himself in, closing the door behind him and locking it. He didn't want to be interrupted.

He walked over to the large portrait of himself, Max and his parents that was situated behind Max's desk. He removed it and leaned it against the wall. Behind it was a safe. He knew it held everything in there from spare cash, personal jewellery items and documents. Most importantly his parents will. Mason turned the dial left then right then left again until he heard the click of the safe opening. Reaching inside he pulled out the will.

'WHAT THE FUCK ARE YOU DOING?' Max's voice bellowed. Mason spun round.

'HOW THE HELL DID YOU GET IN HERE?'

'This is my office Mason and you have no right to be in here. How I got in is irrelevant. Now I will ask again, what the fuck are you doing? Is that dads will in your hand? I suggest you put it the fuck back' Max said through gritted teeth.

'So what if it is. I was just making sure I had all the facts correct before I made a copy of it for my solicitor. I wonder….. does Izzy know that you're using her? I bet she doesn't. I bet you've sweet talked that girl until you got in to her pants. I bet she felt good. Did she feel good brother dear? Was she wet for you? Did you fuck her hard until she.....arrgh'.

Max had stormed across the room within seconds and punched Mason square on the chin, sending him flying back and crashing in to the wall.

Mason rubbed his chin and laughed 'well well, I do believe my brother has fallen for the little tart. I reckon once she knows about your sneaky plan to marry her she won't be so giving' he laughed again and pulled himself up off of the floor, using the wall for support.

'That is not what I am doing Mason. Now put that will back in the safe and leave. In fact I never want to see your face around here ever again, do I make myself clear?'.

Mason studied his brother for a second. Picking up his briefcase off the floor, he pushed the will in to Max's chest as he passed.

'This isn't the end Max, this is just the beginning. I will make sure you suffer, believe me'. Mason turned on his heel and left through the now open door.

Max placed the will back in to the safe and closed the door. He really should change the combination in case Mason sneaked back in and stole it. He was just placing the portrait back on the wall when he heard a tap on the door.

'Hi' Izzy said as she breezed through the door 'Max are you ok? You look like you've seen a ghost'.

'I'm fine' he said. Though he was clearly not. He couldn't risk

Mason telling Izzy anything. His only hope was that his brother would listen for once in his life and never return to the farm.

Max noticed she was carrying two mugs.

'Is one of those for me?' he asked, nodding in the direction of her hands.

'Oh yes here, sorry I was miles away' she walked over to him and handed him one of the mugs 'was that Mason I saw leave?'

Max's eyes widened 'what did he say to you?'.

'Who Mason? Nothing, I just saw him leaving through the front door as I came out of the kitchen. Why has something happened? Is it something serious? Why does it matter if he spoke to me Max? What's going on? You're scaring me now'.

'It's nothing, really. Look, do you want to have a ride in to town with me in a bit? That's if you haven't anything planned with Lorna' he asked.

Izzy shook her head 'no nothing planned, she's down at the cottage with Nick. Those two have become inseparable I must say. So yes is my answer, I would love to come with you. Let me just go freshen up first ok'.

'Sure, just come out to the truck when you're done'.

Max watched her walk out the office. He slumped down in his chair and opened a file to finish off some work.

He couldn't stop thinking about Mason and what he had said. He had to keep him away from Izzy. All he could think of to do was to send her and Lorna away, to convince them to continue on their travels. After all it was what they had come to New Zealand for.

Yes, that was his only option, he decided.

CHAPTER SEVENTEEN

It was a quaint little town. It had a post office, a pub, a supermarket, an eatery and a petrol station. Pretty much everything you needed. The supermarket sold not only food but everything you could think off, from cutlery to canoes. Izzy followed Max in to the supermarket.

'I just need to pick up a few groceries then we can go get something to eat if you want' he suggested.

'Sure, sounds great' Izzy gave him a sideways glance.

'Why don't you take a look around while I get what I need and meet you at the exit' Max said before walking away.

Max was acting weird and Izzy couldn't understand why. He had been quiet on the journey in to town even though she had tried to engage him in conversation, he had merely grunted. Something was off and she needed to know why.

Max took Izzy to a café style eatery called Joes Garage. It was a quaint little place owned by an elderly couple. Joe was the husband and his wife Mave had worked there for Joes parents since she was eighteen. They had met when Joe had returned home from the army on leave. He had taken a real shine to Mave and her to Joe. They had been together ever since.

Izzy and Max sat at the counter and ordered burger and fries.
She stared at the old black and white photo on the wall at the
back of the counter of a young couple stood outside a small
church. They looked so happy, the bride holding her bouquet
looking up at her new husband and him smiling and looking
down at his new bride.

Izzys heart melted for a second before a pang of jealousy
shot through it. Why couldn't she have that? All she ever
wanted was to find a man who would love her as much as
she loved him, but all the men she had come across had been
jerks or idiots or jerks or idio.....oh never mind, she thought.
Mave served them their food. Max picked his up.

'Shall we grab a table?' he asked.

Izzy nodded 'ok'. She followed him to a table tucked away in
the far corner.

'Don't you want to be seen with me or something?' she
queried.

'What? Oh no it's nothing like that, I just thought we could
talk that's all away from prying eyes and ears'.

'Ok, so what do you want to talk about' she asked and then
took a huge bite out of her burger. Max watched her
tentatively. She had ketchup on her lip and the motion of her
tongue licking it sent an electric shock to his groin. For fuck
sake! What the hell is wrong with you Max, he cursed under
his breath at himself.

Izzy looked up 'sorry, what did you say? I didn't hear you'.
Max had to think quickly. 'I was just asking you what

destination you had planned next on your travels'.

She had been about to take another bite of her burger and paused, burger just slightly touching her lips.

'I'm not sure, why?' she said slowly 'are you trying to get rid of us again? Have we over stayed our welcome? I can have a word with Lorna when we get back and be out of your way first thing tomorrow if that's ok because we really don't want to be out when it's dark so I guess this is our last day toge...'

Max reached his hand across and stroked her cheek.

'Stop talking Izzy and I wouldn't dream of letting you leave tonight. I can drop you both off at the bus station in the morning'.

Izzy dropped her burger on the plate and stood up, staring down at Max with disbelief. How could he be so cold towards her? Had the time they have spent together meant nothing to him? Did their love making mean nothing to him? She shook her head at him. All he could do was look at her with sadness in his eyes, but Izzy was fuming and couldn't see that.

'Can we go now please. I need to speak to Lorna'.

'You haven't finished your burger'.

'Yeh well I've just lost my appetite so can we go please'.

Max threw his napkin on the table and got up. He reached out to her but she turned and walked away, he had no option but to follow her all the way back to the truck.

He knew what he was doing was cruel, he knew he had hurt

her, but it was for her own good, at least that's what he thought.

CHAPTER EIGHTEEN

Izzy and Max drove back to the farm in silence. They would both sneak glances at each other. Izzy scowled at him and although Max could feel her glare he kept quiet, after all what could he say to her to make her feel better without doing a three sixty and giving her false hope.

The minute the truck stopped, Izzy jumped out and ran in to the house. Max sighed, he knew he had hurt her but what else could he do, tell her the truth! He shook his head, no way was he going to drag her in to this mess, he would find another way and Mason could go to hell.

Izzy stood in the shower trying to scrub the disgust from her, her skin red raw, stinging from the tears that cascaded down her face. Why was being so mean? She didn't understand it. She heard Lorna call from the bedroom. She got out of the shower and dried herself quickly.

'I won't be long, just having a shower' she shouted through the door. She turned back to the mirror and looked at her sorry reflection. What had happened to her? How could she have fallen for someone so hard and so quick? Why was she allowing herself to be hurt yet again?

She couldn't get Max and his behaviour towards her out of

her head. The little time they had spent together, she thought she knew him pretty well, that he was a decent guy and how he came across was respectful to women. So why was he behaving like a complete knob head now! Something was off she knew that much, she also knew she wouldn't be treated like this anymore, not by him or any other man she might date in the future. No, now was the time to take a stand. She would take a stand and give him what for.

She stood up straight, pulling her shoulders back and her head up high, she wrapped the towel tight around her and purposefully walked out of the bathroom.

Lorna was sat on the bed taking off her shoes.

'Hey are we.....Izzy what's happened?'

'Nothing why?' Izzy busied herself getting dressed by the wardrobe with a determination she had never felt before.

'Because your face looks like thunder, that's why. What's going on chick?' Lorna had stopped what she was doing and turned to face her.

'I am sick to death of been treated like a door mat that's what. Max wants shut of us so we're going first thing. Right now though I am going to confront him and find out what is going on because I will not be treated like shit, not by him or anyone else for that matter'.

The surprised look on Lorna face was a picture. She had never heard or seen her friend like this before. Something bad must have happened because this wasn't her friend at all. She was so used to Izzy been placid and accepting of the knob heads behaviour with whom she had dated over the years. Maybe now finally she had realised she was better than that and from now on will stand up for herself and not put up with being treated like dirt. Good on her, she thought.

'Would you like me there for back up?' Lorna asked.

'No, this is something I have to do myself. Start as I mean to go on sort of thing'.

'Ok Izzykins, I'll be waiting right here'.

CHAPTER NINETEEN

Izzy was about to knock on Max's study door when she heard him talking. She couldn't make out if he was on the phone or someone else was there. Maybe it was Nick or maybe Mason had come back. She pressed her ear against the door to try and get a better listen. She couldn't hear anything now.
Damn it.
The door swung open, startling her and she fell straight in to Max's arms.
'What the hell! Izzy what are you doing?'
'I …. Sorry. I was just about to knock on the door when you opened it. We need to talk and I am NOT taking no for an answer or any cocked up story as to why you can't talk….. also i…'.
Max lowered his head and kissed her hard before releasing her.
'Yes, we will talk, but not now. There's something I need to do first. I have to go out of town for a few days, but when I get back we will talk and I will tell you everything'. He kissed her again and walked away, leaving her stood there open mouthed as she watched him ascend the stairs.
It took her a minute to snap out of her daze and when she did, Lorna was standing in front of her, wafting Izzy's face

with her hand.

'Hey chick, are you ok? What happened with lover boy?'

'Huh? Oh that, nothing happened. I mean, he said he had to go out of town for a few days and that we would talk when he gets back. So I guess we won't be going anywhere just yet. At least you get to spend more time with Nick'.

Lorna studied her friend intently. 'You don't think he's playing you for a fool Izzy? I mean he's been blowing hot and cold since we got here. Could him going away just be another delaying ploy?'

'No, I don't think so. I think he really means what he says. I think he does really have feelings for me but just too scared to tell me or actually do anything about it. No, whatever he has to go away and sort out has to do with me. I don't know what or why but I just know it has'.

'I hope your right chick. I hate seeing you hurting, but if he does hurt you I will kick his ass big time!'

Izzy laughed 'Thanks Lorna, I know you got my back'.

Max came down carrying an overnight bag. He had got changed into a navy blue suit, white shirt and navy blue striped tie. His hair had been sleeked backed.

Both Izzy and Lorna admiring eyes made him chuckle.

He dropped the bag on the floor and walked over to Izzy.

'I promise I won't be long and I promise we will talk when I get back' he leaned in and kissed her cheek.

'Nick will be here holding the fort so let him know if you need anything. I'm sure you'll take good care of her for me Lorna, that I can rest assure. One more thing ladies, if Mason should attempt to enter the house while I am away, call Nick, he will handle it ok. Well I had better make tracks, see you in a few days ladies'.

They watched him pick up his bag and walk out the door, before closing it he popped his head back round 'Keep this door locked while I'm away. Bye'.

CHAPTER TWENTY

Max paced the floor. He hated lawyers. He hated having to be here and do what he was about to do, but he couldn't let Mason get his own way and take away everything from him. There had to be a loophole somewhere in his fathers will, that at least would stop everything going to his brother if he couldn't marry before the time is up! Damn him. He cursed his father for his stupid rules.

He spun round when he heard the door open.

'Hello Mr Veto. Please take a seat. I have all the paperwork here'.

Max sat down but couldn't relax, he needed to know what the lawyer had found out.

'So having reviewed all the paperwork Mr Veto, I'm sorry to have to tell you that I found nothing that can help you. The will is water tight. Contesting the will isn't an option either I'm afraid' he sat back in his chair and stared at Max for moment 'I knew your father for thirty years. He was good at what he did, hardworking, a fantastic business man, but when he had me draw up his will, I had to question his thinking and his ethics. After all you're both his sons. I tried to reason with him about the clause he had placed on you to marry. I really wished I could have talked him out of it, but he was a stubborn old coot. Sorry I couldn't be more help Max, I really am'.

'I guess I have only one option left'.

The lawyer raised a quizzical eyebrow and Max shook his head and laughed.

Max left the lawyers offices feeling a little deflated. The talk he was going to have with Izzy when he got back wasn't the one he was originally going to have with her. Now he had to lie to her, not about how he felt, that was true enough, but because now he would have to ask her to marry him and not tell her the real reason why they had to do it in the next couple of weeks. His only hope now was that she would say yes to his proposal. She had feelings for him that much he knew. He just prayed that it was enough that she would marry him.

He lay awake most of the night thinking what he was going to say to Izzy, how he was going to propose. It's not like he can walk in the door and say "hi Izzy, fancy getting married to me?" No, he had to play it clever. If he was to do it right, he had to take his time and not rush it, well not too much any way.

CHAPTER TWENTY-ONE

Lorna was spending the day with Nick in own. They had asked if she wanted to go, but Izzy didn't feel like been a third wheel and sent them on their way, assuring them both she would be fine on her own. She wanted to fully explore the farm and go for a swim in the lake, it was a hot day and she needed to cool down.

She grabbed her bathing suit and a towel then headed out, she would have a swim and then a saunter about.

By the lake she stripped down naked, feeling comfortable in the knowledge she was all alone. She put on her bikini and slowly edged in to the water. God it felt good. The cool temperature of the water was bliss on her hot skin. She swam across to the little island where Max had taken her to and managed after a few attempts to pull herself up.

Laying back on the grass to soak up the sun, she drifted off in to slumber. She dreamed of the last time she was here with Max, how they had sex and how good it felt.

She jumped up with a start out of her sleep when she heard rustling in the bushes. A little fearful of what it could be, she edged towards the water, ready to jump in and swim back to shore. 'Hello, who's there? Hello?' she called out but no-one answered. She started to panic a little and was about to jump in to the water until she saw what came out from under the bush. A possum! Her shoulders dropped with relief, but then she remembered they could be snappy little shits. It was time for her to go, she decided and jumped in to the water and swam back to shore.

Picking up her towel, she stripped off her bikini and was drying off when she heard a noise behind her. Looking back she saw nothing and shrugged her shoulders thinking it was probably another possum.

She continued to dry herself off, bending over to dry her legs, she hadn't realised someone stood behind her. Grabbing her and throwing her to the ground, she screamed and tried to cover her naked body with the towel, but they ripped it from her grasp. She kicked out at them but to no avail, they straddled her and pinned her arms above her head. Her eyes closed, she moved her head from side to side screaming before they placed a hand over her mouth to mute her.

'Shut the fuck up, I am not going to hurt you, you stupid bitch'.

She slowly opened her eyes at the familiar sounding voice.

'If I remove my hand, will you be quiet?'

Izzy nodded. They removed their hand.

'Mason!'

CHAPTER TWENTY-TWO

She squealed at the top of her voice, but no-one could hear her. No-one was coming to rescuing her. No-one even knew she was here, only Mason who had locked her in. It felt like she had been there for days, even though she knew it was hours.

Mason had made her get dressed and then marched her or about 3 miles to an abandoned cave. It had large wooden doors to the entrance, that once closed didn't let any light in what so ever. Now I know what solitary confinement feels like, she had thought.

He had said nothing to her as to why he was doing this and only spoke to tell her to keep walking and to get in the cave. She was sure that once Lorna got back and realised her friend was missing she contact Max and they would search for her. All she had to do was to sit and wait.

She slumped back against the wall, exhausted from shouting and screaming help.

Hang on a minute, she thought. What if the reason he put her in here was because he knew that no-one would ever find her? What if he's a secret murderer? Max wouldn't have known, after all he doesn't get along with his brother.

She wondered how many more people Mason had brought

here and been left to die. Fuck! What if she was standing or sitting on bones from dead people! She started to panic, adrenalin kicked in and jumping up, she started pounding on the door again.

'Let me out of here, please Mason let me out. I promise I won't tell anyone what you have done. Max need never know. I won't say anything. Please Mason, just let me go'. She took a step back when she heard the door being unlocked.

Light flooding the cave as the door opened and Mason stepped inside.

'Tell me Ms Cruz, how exactly do you know what I have done? Did you find something on one of your snoops? Tell me now Isabella'.

She gasped. What was he on about? He had obviously done something other than locking her in here and thinks she knows about it.

What would be the best option? To deny knowing anything, because in fact that would be the truth or to pretend she knew whatever it was he thinks she knows? The latter would probably keep her locked up, but who's to say he wouldn't anyway if she denied knowing anything? Whatever she said, she needed to say it now, because the look on his face was getting angrier by the second.

'I know everything ok. So I suggest you let me go and we can work something out'. What the hell just came out of her mouth? What the hell is she thinking?

Mason studied her for a minute. What was the bitch playing at? He thought she was this sickly sweet and innocent silly cow. Maybe he has underestimated her. Maybe she could an ally? Or maybe she's just playing games and knows nothing so I will let her go! He would test her.

'So, what did you have in mind?'

Shit, he was calling her bluff. She nervously licked her lips and said the first thing that came in to her head '50/50 or I tell Max everything'.

She knows! Fuck! He had two options. He could either just leave her rot or go along with it. The latter seemed the better option, at least then farm wouldn't be swarmed with cops and such looking for her and then finding her body, especially since he had man handled her, so his DNA was all over her. He had to trust in what she said. Damn her! He would be negotiating 50/50 though.

'Ok Isabella, we have a deal, but at 60/40, after all I am the one doing the hard work, so to speak. So, do we have a deal?'

Izzy sighed with relief and nodded.

Stepping aside, Mason let her pass, grabbing her arm as she reached the door 'Don't let me down. By the way, when did you know what I was doing?'

'I won't and it was on my second day here. Now can I go back to the farm, I need to take a shower'.

He let go of her arm and watched her walk towards his car.

CHAPTER TWENTY-THREE

Izzy came running down the stairs as the door opened. Max walked in and dropped his bag to the floor as Izzy threw herself at him.

'Oh Max, I am so glad your back' before he could think she planted a kiss on his lips. How could he resist. He wrapped his arms around her waist and kissed her back.

Finally drawing breath he said 'well that was some welcome home, I could get used to this. I missed you too. How's everything been while I've been away?'

'Everything has been ok. Lorna and Nick have just nipped for groceries, she's cooking dinner later so I hope you've got some antacid' she pulled a face and Max laughed.

'Is she that bad of a cook?'

'Well put it this way, she can burn water'.

He laughed again, unwrapping his arms from her waist and picking up his bag 'Is that even possible?'

'You would be surprised. Anyway, how was your trip? Good I hope'.

'Could have gone better, but nothing for you to worry about. I need a shower and a change of clothes, so catch you in a bit'. He kissed her on the tip of her nose and headed upstairs, taking them two by two.

Izzy made her way in to living room and to the bar in the corner of the room. She fixed both Max and herself a drink. Staring in to the bottom of her glass, she pondered whether to tell him about what happened with Mason, and then thought better of it.

After what Mason had done the other day, she had decided she was going to find out what it was exactly he was hiding from Max. Once she found that out, she could tell Max everything.

She looked up when Max entered the room and smiled. She still couldn't believe her luck that he fancied her as much as she him. He gave her butterflies every time he walking in to a room, every time he looked at her.

'First a lovely welcome home and now fixing me a drink, I really could get used to this. So tell me, what have you been up to while I was away? Come and sit with me'. He walked over to the large sofa and sat down, patting the seat beside him. Izzy carried their drinks over and handed him his before sitting down.

'Nothing much really. I had a swim in the lake and a walk around the grounds. I love it here; I wish I didn't have to leave'.

His glass stopped, just as it touched his lips.

'You're leaving?'

'What? Oh I don't mean right now I mean in the next couple of weeks. I think we may have out stayed our welcome'.

'Izzy, you could never out stay your welcome. In fact, I would love it if you stayed for the rest of your trip. I mean that's if you want to, you and Lorna that is'.

She turned to face him. She couldn't think of anything else she would rather do.

'I… I mean we, we would love to stay. Thanks Max. I suppose I was hoping you say that. Fuck it…love it or lose it. Max, recently I have been having, well, I mean lately I have had these feelings. What I mean is…..' he was smiling at her '….Anyway like I was saying, these feelings, well….' Max placed a finger on her lips.

'I feel the same Izzy' he stroked her bottom lip with his finger, sending electrifying shivers throughout her body. Leaning in, he kissed her gently.

Could this be really happening? Did he just say he loved her? Wait, no, he didn't, but then she hadn't said it to him either. She pulled away.

'What do you mean you feel the same?'

'I've fallen or you Isabella Cruz. I didn't want to say anything before because I didn't want to scare you off. I guess I was waiting for you to say it first. I didn't want you to feel obligated to stay if I had told you how I felt'.

'You silly sausage' she laughed, wrapping her arms around his neck and kissing him.

CHAPTER TWENTY-FOUR

Izzy realised the key to finding out what Mason up to, was in Max's study. He was going in to town soon so that was her chance to get in there and have a look to see what she could find. He always kept it locked but she had told him she needed to use the phone to ring back to England and as that was the only room with a phone, he said he would leave it unlocked for her.

After Max had left, she made her way to his study. It was unlocked like he said. She closed the door behind her and went to the window to check and make sure no-one was about. Lorna had gone to Nick's cottage but she wasn't sure how long she would be. Confident she was alone she began searching Max's desk first, careful not to disturb all the paperwork that was strewn all over his desk. It was nothing exciting, just stuff to do with stock deliveries for cattle and the such. She checked the book case next, but again she found nothing.

She stood scratching her head. She had looked everywhere she could think of.

She was about to turn and leave when the picture on the wall behind his desk caught her eye. The picture was crooked. Now anyone who knew her, knew she was a little o.c.d.

Izzy went over to the picture and lifted her hand to straighten it, then stopped. Something shiny was behind it. She lifted the picture off of the wall and placed it on the floor, leaning it against the wall. She stood back to take in the imposing safe before her. Damn it! She bet that whatever she needed to know, was locked in that safe. Shit! Now what was she going to do?

She placed the picture back and left the study. She had to think of something to get in to that safe!

CHAPTER TWENTY-FIVE

Tonight was the night, Max thought. He would set the stage so to speak. Candle lit dinner, a dusk walk through the meadow. He would set up a blanket with champagne and strawberries by the lake with lit candles and then he would ask her to marry him. He prayed she would say yes. He knew it was a rush but he knew she had feelings for him and him her, so why wait. At least that is what he would say to her, why wait!

Izzy sauntered in to the living room. Max had his back to her sat on the sofa, he was going through some paperwork and hadn't heard her enter the room.

She stood quietly watching him. Her heart skipped and flipped as she stared at the back of his head. Now she was just being pathetic! How can the back of someone's head give you goose bumps? Because you are in love with him that's why, dozy cow!

Max must have sensed someone stood behind him and turned, smiling when he saw it was Izzy.

'Why are you stood there? Come and sit with me' he said, patting the seat beside him. 'So how long have you been standing there?' he asked.

'Oh, not long. How long have you been sat here?' she asked.

'Oh, not long' Max replied, laughing and grabbing hold her head, he pulled her close and kissed her warmly. Izzy sunk in to his arms and groaned.

Pulling away, he looked deep in to her eyes and licked his lips. He had to say it. He had to tell her now how he felt. 'Isabella, I love you. I mean, I have fallen in love with you....' she was about to speak, but he placed a finger gently on her lips '....please, let me finish. I know we haven't known each other very long, but I have never felt like this for anyone. You crashed in to my life and made an almighty dint. The first time I saw you, it was like I had been hit by a bus full of love. You gave me butterflies from the instant I saw you and god, when you looked at me with those eyes, those beautiful big brown eyes. Well let's just say I needed a couple of cold showers' he giggled, looking down. He took hold of her hand and brought it up to his mouth, kissing her palm.

'I love you too Max' Izzy rushed her words out. She had sat as quietly as possible, but she wanted to say to him everything he had said to her. She was fidgeting and couldn't hold it in any longer.

They ate a fabulous dinner. A starter of scallops on a bed of rocket salad, and then steak with chunky chips with creamy mushroom sauce. Dessert would come later.

As planned, Max took Izzy for a walk through the meadow and down to the lake. As they reached the edge of the clearing he stopped and pulled her close.

'I have a surprise for you. Close your eyes'. He lifted her

hands up to her face, positioning them over her eyes. Izzy giggled with excitement, she loved surprises.

'What is it?'

'Now if I told you, it wouldn't be a surprise would it. Now shush and close your eyes. I will guide you'.

He guided her path towards the blanket, then released her.

'Ok, you can open your eyes now'.

When she did and saw what lay before her, she squealed with delight.

There was a mug with a bunch of beautiful red roses inside. Two champagne flutes, a bottle of champagne and a bowl of fresh strawberries. So fresh in fact she could smell there sweet aroma.

'Wow. I mean..... wow. I can't believe you've done all this for little old me. You are sweet'.

'It's what you deserve. Here, sit with me'. Max sat on the blanket with his legs crossed and picking up the bottle of champagne, he popped the cork and poured them each a glass.

Izzy helped herself to one of the large juicy strawberries.

'I could get used to this every day' she lay back and let out a little groan of satisfaction.

'Don't you think you would get bored if you did this every day?' he asked.

'Huh! No way' she chuckled and perched on her elbow facing him. 'So what's with all this seduction malarkey anyway? You do remember we have already had sex, don't you?'

Max let out a heavy sigh. He took hold of her free hand and pulled her up to face him. He brushed a loose strand from face and tucked it behind her ear.

'Not everything is about sex Izzy. I did all this because I love you and I wanted to show you how much....' he paused, taking a couple of deep breaths '....i can't believe I am doing this. I never thought this day would ever arrive but......' he paused again and began rummaging in his trouser pocket.

Izzy's eyes widened 'Errm, Max, what are you doing?'

Max cursed under his breath as he struggled and grappled with something inside his pocket.

'One moment please' he said, standing up to get better access. He yanked whatever it was so hard from his pocket, that it left the grip of his fingers and went flying in to the lake.

Izzy stood, mouth gaping. 'What the hell was that?'

Max turned the air blue. Izzy figured he had used every profanity known to man in the space of thirty seconds.

'Stay there' he said and began undressing.

Izzy stood speechless as she watched him strip down to his boxer shorts and dive in to the water.

He came up for air a couple of times before eventually coming out of the water, with what looked like a small box gripped tightly in his hand.

Dripping wet, he shook the excess water from his hair and knelt down in front of her.

Izzy was frozen to the spot. Her mind rushing thoughts

through her head. Was he really going to do what she thought he was going to do? Mind racing and mouth dry, she tried to rush the pros and cons of saying yes before she decided what she would, should say.

Max took hold of her hand and looked up at her.

OH SHIT! She thought. What is she going to say?

'Izzy, my darling, this isn't how I wanted it to go, I guess best laid plans and all that, but would you do me the honour of marrying me.......please?'

CHAPTER TWENTY-SIX

Lorna stretched out on the couch. She loved spending time with Nick. They knew it would only be a holiday romance, they had both made that clear from the start. Neither one of them were looking for anything other than a bit of fun.
Nick had been gone a while. He said he was going to take a quick shower then make them both something to eat.
She checked her watch; he had been in the shower for almost an hour. What was keeping him? She thought. Her tummy rumbled. She decided she could wait no longer and went in search for him. As she stood up, she heard a loud thud. What the hell was that! It had come from upstairs. Had Nick slipped while getting out of the shower? What if he was hurt? She wasted no time and headed towards the stairs. When she reached the foot of the stairs, she could hear a groan then what sounded like something being dragged along the floor.
'NICK, ARE YOU OK? ARE YOU HURT? SHOULD I GO AND GET HELP?' Lorna shouted up the stairs. Her heart was beating fast and hard. She was fearful now because he wasn't answering, not to mention the strange noises.
She put a foot on the bottom step and held on to the banister, she looked up the stairs in to the darkness but

couldn't see anything. She was about to call out again but thought better of it when she heard another strange sound. It was like a dying dog whimpering for mercy.

Now she was petrified. Something was up there with Nick and he was possibly, probably hurt but whatever it was she wasn't about to find out for herself. She turned on her heel and scarpered out of the front door. She realised half way up the path she was bare foot. Fuck that! She thought and ran all the way back up the dirt track towards the farm house. She figured Izzy and Max would be there and accompany her back to Nick's cottage to check on him.

She didn't look back once and when she reached the farm house, other than the porch lights been on, the rest of the house was in total darkness. Fuck, fuck and fuck again, she shouted in her head.

She tried the door but it was locked. She looked back in the direction of the cottage and saw what can only be described as a giant orange ball. What the hell! Slowly realising that actually, the cottage was engulfed in flames.

She dropped to her knees 'NICK, NO. NICK PLEASE. OH GOD NO. NICK' she cried out at the top of her lungs.

She reached in her jeans pocket for her phone, dropping it on to the ground because her hands were shaking.

She managed to swipe the screen and bring up contacts, she scrolled down to Izzy's number and dialled. Nothing. She tried again, no answer. She then remembered she had saved the New Zealand emergency services number in to her phone before they had flown, after googling it just in case they needed it. She scrolled down again and found 111 and pressed dial.

'Hello, what service do you require please?' the lady asked.

'It's my boyfriend's cottage, well he's not actually my boyfriend but ….. I mean sorry. I need fire & ambulance, the cottage is on fire and I think he's still inside' Lorna rushed her words out.

'Ok, try and stay calm. Can you tell me your name miss?'

'WHAT! MY NAME, YOU WANT TO KNOW MY FUCKING NAME WHEN MY BOYFRIEND IS PROBABLY BURNED TO A CRISP BY NOW. JUST SEND A FUCKING FIRE ENGINE AND AMBULANCE TO THE VETO FARM AND HURRY THE FUCK UP'.

Lorna pressed the end call button and turned back to watch the cottage burning.

Why wasn't Izzy answering her phone? More to the point why was the whole house in darkness?

She could do no more. She sat on the top step of the porch and waited. It must have been thirty-five minutes before she heard sirens. She jumped up and ran back down the dirt track towards the two fire trucks that were pulling up.

The officer in charge saw her and stopped her going any further.

'Miss, you have stay here' he said, spreading his arms out so she couldn't pass.

'Please my boyfriend is in there. You have to get him out' she was out of breath and gasping in between words.

'We're doing everything we can Miss, but you have to stay here. Maybe you can help us by telling me if you know how it started'.

Lorna slumped her shoulders. She had suddenly become exhausted.

'Here take a seat Miss, you look like you're about to collapse'. He helped her towards a tree stump that was perfectly shaped to sit on.

She took a deep breath 'I'm not really sure what happened to be honest. One minute I was laying on the sofa and Nick...that's my boyfriend, he was in the shower, but he was taking too long so I went to check on him and that's when I heard......' she drifted off, staring beyond the officer. He followed her gaze. Two firemen were carrying a body bag and it wasn't an empty one.

Lorna stared. She was in shock. The officer called out to a paramedic as they opened the back doors to the ambulance for the firemen to gain access with the body bag.

'I think she's gone in to shock, take her in will you' the officer said. The paramedic nodded and helped Lorna to her feet and guided her towards the second ambulance that had just pulled up.

'Hey Bob, can you take care of this lady, she's gone in to shock'.

Lorna rode in the ambulance to the hospital in silence, staring at the vehicles inside walls. She wrapped the blanket what the paramedic had given her, tightly around her.

Was that Nicks body they had carried out? It had to be didn't it? Who else could it have been? No-one else was in the house other than them. Then she remembered the noises. Someone else WAS in the cottage!

CHAPTER TWENTY-SEVEN

Max and Izzy rounded the corner holding hands. They hadn't heard the sirens or seen the blaze or even felt the heat from the flames. They had been in their own little world.

They were stopped dead in their tracks though when they finally managed to drag their eyes from each other and look up.

The firemen had finally got the fire under control and most of it was now out. There were just a few small fires dotted about which would be put out in no time.

The cottage was a shell. No more roof, no more walls, just smouldering cinders.

Max let go of Izzy's hand and raced down to the fire officer standing by one of the fire trucks.

'What the hell happened here? Is anyone hurt?' He rushed his words as adrenalin kicked in.

'Are you the owner?'

'Yes, I own the farm and this cottage. Was anyone hurt? My friend and his girlfriend are staying here'.

'I'm afraid we did find the body of a male. His girlfriend has been taken to the hospital, she wasn't hurt but she was suffering from shock'.

Max ran a hand over his face. 'What happened? Was it an

accident or arson?.

'Sorry but at this time we don't know anything. Right now the best thing you can do is go to the hospital and speak to your friend's girlfriend. She seemed confused when I questioned her earlier. Maybe you can get some sense out of her'.

Max took out his wallet and took a business card out of it and handed it to the fire officer.

'If you find anything out, please contact me. I need to know what happened'.

The officer nodded, taking the card from him 'I will sir'.

Izzy hadn't moved. She was stunned at the sight before her. She knew Lorna was spending the night at Nicks. She needed to go and see if they were ok but she couldn't move, it was if she was glued to the ground. Her whole body was stiff. She couldn't even cry out, her lips wouldn't even move. Her mind raced, nothing making any sense. Where is Lorna? Where is my best friend? Why hadn't Max come back to her? He must know something, she had seen him speaking to the fire officer but he was still standing there, staring at the cottage. She tried to move her feet, but they wouldn't budge.

For fucks sake Izzy, come on, your friend was in there now get moving. She tried again but was firmly stuck to the spot. She was trying to shuffle her feet in the dirt when someone grabbed her hand. She looked up. It was Max. at that moment she felt weak and fainted in to his arms. Max swooped her up and carried her to the porch. He wrestled in his pocket for the door keys.

When they got inside, he carried her in to the living room and laid her on the sofa.

Izzy let out a low groan.

Max stroked her hair. 'Shh darling, everything will be ok'.

He knew he was lying. How could what had happened be ok? He would get to the bottom of it, whatever it takes. For now, though he would be here for Izzy. For now, that's what was important and after she had rested, they would go to the hospital and check on Lorna.

CHAPTER TWENTY-EIGHT

Lorna was feeling sorry for herself sat alone in the hospital cubicle. The doctor who had examined her had told her she had to stay in overnight for observation. She had tried to argue that she felt fine now, but the doctor replied "you've had a very nasty shock Miss Regan and we need to keep an eye on you and make sure you are what you say you are. Fine!" So she nodded, laid back and closed her eyes.

She tried to go through in her mind everything that had happened tonight. Had there been someone else in the cottage? Had they already been there when her and Nick had got back from town or broke in when they were already home? What exactly were the noises she had heard?

She tried to remember. A thud and then a scraping, dragging noise as if something or someone was being dragged across the floor. The groaning, like someone was hurt, in pain. Why would anyone want to hurt them or maybe it was Nick who was the intended victim.

Tears streamed down her cheeks as she also remembered the firemen carrying out a body bag. Nick. She couldn't believe what had happened. Then she started to blame herself. If we hadn't come to New Zealand, then none of this would have happened. Nick would still be alive.

She put her head in her hands and sobbed, then looked up when she heard the curtain to the cubicle draw back.

'Izzy!'

Izzy ran over to her and hugged her tightly. 'I'm sorry I couldn't get here any sooner; I was in shock. I've been so worried. I thought I had lost you when I saw the fire. What happened Lorna? Max told me about Nick, I'm so sorry'.

'I don't know. I'm so confused. I heard things, strange things' she lowered her voice 'I think someone was in the cottage, I think someone hurt Nick and I didn't know what to do. Izzy it's all my fault. Why didn't I do something? Why didn't I go upstairs when I heard noises? Nick might still be alive now if I just had the courage instead of being scared and running away'.

Izzy put her hand up 'Stop that right now, do you hear me. If you had done that, gone up stairs, then that someone might have hurt you too and we wouldn't be here talking right now. I don't know what I would do without you; you're my best friend, like a sister. So no more of this blaming yourself ok because none of this is your fault'.

Max popped his head around the curtain 'Hi Lorna, how are you doing?'

The girls looked round and smiled, but it was Izzy who spoke. 'She's going to be ok, thanks Max'.

Just then Lorna squealed and grabbed Izzy hand and pointing at it.

'Is that what I think it is?' she asked, pulling Izzy's hand towards her for a closer inspection of the glistening rock perched on her ring finger.

Izzy giggled 'Yes it is, but now is not the time or place. We will talk later when the time is right and you're feeling better ok. I'm just going to go and talk to Max for a minute but I will be right back ok. Try and get some rest'.

Lorna nodded, laid back and closed her eyes. she felt exhausted so it wasn't long before she drifted off to sleep. Izzy kissed her forehead and left the cubicle, following Max down the corridor to a drinks vending machine.

'Can I get you a coffee?' he asked. Izzy shook her head. He could see the worry in her face.

'Hey, she will be alright you know....' He paused and studied Izzys face. 'Did she say anything? About what happened I mean'.

'She says she's confused, that she heard noises upstairs but was too scared to go up. I think she thinks that Nick was murdered and then the cottage set alight to hide it. Max, I don't know what I would have done in her situation; I think I would have run as far away from there as possible too'.

'That is what I would have wanted you to do and I am pretty sure Nick felt that way too. I'm sure if he could have done, he would have shouted for Lorna to get out of the cottage and to safety. I'm just sorry we weren't there when she needed us'. He sat down on the chair beside her and held her hand in his.

'I promise you I will find out who did this. Will you be ok here with Lorna for a while? I have to go and identify Nick's body. A prospect I am not looking forward to but his family live north. Shit! I need to notify them'. He scraped his fingers through his hair. Izzy leaned in and kissed his cheek.

'You do what you need to do, I'll be fine here with Lorna.

'Max ……'

'Yes'.

'I love you'.

'I love you too Izzy, more than you'll ever know'.

He kissed the back of her hand. She stared at his back as he walked off down the corridor.

CHAPTER TWENTY-NINE

Max was dreading having to identify his friend's body. The only other dead body he had ever seen had been his parents in their open caskets.

He headed hastily towards the morgue. The sooner he got it over with the better.

A police officer and a morgue technician were stood outside two large white doors when Max approached.

'Excuse me, my names Max Veto. I was told I needed to come and identify my friend's body'.

Both men stopped talking and turned to face Max, looking him up and down.

'What name is it' the tech asked.

'Nick Elliot'.

'Follow me'. The tech nodded at the police officer then pushed one of the large white doors open. Max followed.

The tech took him into a room and told him to wait there. He scanned the room, the room was stark to say the least, nothing in it but a rectangle shaped table in the middle of the room. The walls were grey, some of the paint had chipped off the walls. On one wall there was a small window with drawn curtains on the other side of it. Fuck me, he thought. This room was depressing! But then what did he expect what with it been a morgue. It was hardly going to have brightly painted walls and soft furnishings, though a chair would have been nice, a practical touch, he thought.

The tech returned and asked Max to stand in front of the curtained window.

'Mr Veto, I must warn you first of the condition of the body. It was badly burned and any description of your friend will help with fully identifying the body. Now all you need to do is tell me when you are ready and I will notify Bill in the viewing room to draw back the curtains'.

Max took a deep breath and nodded 'Ok I'm ready'.

The tech tapped on the window. The curtains slowly drew back.

Max let out a loud gasp. His eyes widened. He winced and turned away. He couldn't look, yet couldn't unsee what he had seen.

Was that really his best friend laying there? He wasn't sure.

'Mr Veto, I understand this is difficult, but if there is anything you can see on the body that could identify who it is.....' the tech placed a reassuring hand on Max's shoulder.

Max knew he had no choice but to look again. He had to know for sure. Because if it wasn't Nick, then where the hell was he?

Turning round, he had his eyes closed at first, and then slowly opened them. His heart was pounding hard.

Starting from the head, he intently stared and tried to take in every detail. But the hair was completely burned off and the face had melted beyond recognition. He slowly worked his way down the body, but nothing was recognisable, that is until he reached body's feet. There was still remnants of a pair of shoes.

'His shoes......' Max said, pointing at the body's feet.

The tech looked at where he was pointing.

'What about his feet Mr Veto?'

'It looks like he's wearing leather shoes....and there on his wrist...' he pointed again, this time to a watch on the body's arm '....it looks like a metal strap. Nick didn't wear leather shoes and the only watch I know he owned was a diver's watch and that had a plastic strap'.

'Are you saying that you don't think that man is your friend?' the tech looked at Max and then back to the burned remains laid out on the table.

'No, I am saying without a doubt, that man there is not my friend Nick Elliot'.

'Right well I guess the question is who is that man'.

'No' Max said. 'The question is, where the hell is Nick, and what the hell was my brother doing in the cottage!'

'I'm sorry I don't understand. Your brother?' the tech gave Max a questioning look.

'Yes my brother Mason Veto. That is who you have laying on the table in what I can only describe as THE MOST MISERABLE DEPRESSING FUCKING PLACE ON THIS PLANET' Max lost his cool now. He couldn't breathe, he needed to get out of there and get some air. He loosened his tie and hurried out of the room and down the corridor towards the nearest exit.

His parents were dead and now his brother too. He had lost everything he ever cared about.

He felt a hand on his shoulder and looked up, shielding the glare of the sun with his hand.

'Are you ok? I was getting worried so came looking for you. The morgue man told me you had took off. Was it ..... you know?'

Max couldn't help but smile at Izzy's morgue man term.

'In answer to your questions, I will be and yes, it was you know'. Max stood up straight from the railing he had be leaning on.

'It's not Nick' he admitted to Izzy.

'What ... how.... I mean... oh I don't know what I mean'.

'It's ok I was stunned too. The man in there.....' he nodded in the direction of the hospital '.....was wearing a leather shoes and a watch with a metal strap'.

'And Nick doesn't wear those things I take it'.

Max shook his head 'No but my brother does'.

Izzy hand went to her mouth as she gasped at Max's revelation.

CHAPTER THIRTY

It had been two weeks since the fire. There had still been no sign of Nick. Max constantly rang his phone, but it always went to voice mail so he had left countless messages, pleading for him to get in contact.

The police at least had stopped bothering him, Izzy and Lorna. The constant questioning about Nick, Mason and the fire was becoming to the point of harassment. Max had also enlisted a private detective to find Nick.

The only conclusion everyone had was that for whatever reason Nick had started the fire.

The police and coroner were working on properly identifying the body in the morgue. Skin scrapes and bloods had been and an autopsy performed to determine exactly how he had died.

The only thing they could do right now was to try and carry on the best they could.

Izzy towelled off her hair. She had needed that hot shower. Lorna was curled up asleep on the bed. She tip toed across the bedroom and picked up her dressing gown from the chair in the corner. She turned and watched her friend for a while.

She felt for Lorna loss, because she knew if it had been Max she would have been beside herself. Lorna hadn't been in love with Nick but she had found a kindred spirit which for Lorna was the next best thing.

Izzy tied the dressing gown belt tightly and quietly opened the bedroom door and let herself out. She padded across the soft carpet across the landing towards Max's bedroom and lightly tapped on the door.

'Come in' Max called out.

Izzy entered and softly closed the door behind her.

'Hey, how's Lorna doing?'

'She's sleeping....again! I'm so worried about her and I don't know what to do'.

'Just be there for her like you are already doing. She will let you know what she needs when she's ready. Now come here and lay with me' he patted the space on the bed beside him.

Izzy skipped over and jumped on to the bed. She placed her head on his chest, running her hand across his abdomen.

She could feel his chest rise and fall as he breathed deeply. There was anticipation in the air and it was starting to feel uncomfortable.

Max couldn't hold it in any longer, he had to be honest with her about everything.

'Izzy, there is something I have been meaning to tell you....' he placed a finger on her lips when she raised her head and was about to say speak '..... No, let me finish please, because if I don't say it now, I may never say it and its big Izzy, big and very important. I need you to listen ok and not say a word until I have finished, ok'.

She nodded and listened.

CHAPTER THIRTY-ONE

Izzy sat at the edge of the bed shaking her head in disbelief. Her head started to spin, her breathing becoming more erratic. She couldn't believe what Max had just told her. Not knowing what to think or feel she had started to have a panic attack.

'Izzy please stay calm, I .....'.

'STAY CALM. STAY CALM. ARE YOU FUCKING KIDDING ME!' She screamed at him and jumped up. Max grabbed her arm.

'Please Izzy, I love you'.

She shrugged his arm off and headed for the bedroom door. Stopping, she turned to him 'I can't believe you used me like that, but worse of all I can't believe I let you. I'm such an idiot'.

Max climbed off the bed and went over to her. He searched her face. He wanted to make this right. He wanted to hold her close. He knew the mood she was in right now though; to touch her would make her bolt out that door and that was the last thing he wanted to happen.

He had to prove to her that he really was in love with her and that what his father had stipulated in his will wasn't the reason he had asked her to marry him. But to try and reason with her or try to explain properly to her at this moment was a waste of time, because she wasn't ready to listen to anything. She will need time and space to get her head around what he had told her. The last thing he wanted was to push her away and make her run. No, he would give her that time and space she will need.

'Listen, I know what I told you was, well I know it doesn't sound good, so until you're ready to listen to me, I will give you some time and space to think things through. Just don't leave, please, not until you have heard me out, ok?'

Izzy stood looking up at him, her arms crossed across her chest. A stubborn aura emanating from her. Should she give him the benefit of the doubt? How could she trust him after his revelation? She loved him, that much was true, but how could she be sure that he really loved her?

'Ok Max, I'll stay but I need time to think. I expect my privacy though, so please leave me alone'.

Max inclined his head in acceptance.

Izzy left the room, closing the door quietly behind her.

MASON

Mason had always lived in his brother's shadow. He always felt second best and thought their parents favoured Max over him. Truthfully speaking, none of what he thought was true. His parents Kim and Dave would bend over backwards for their troublesome son.

Max was apparently the golden child in his parent's eyes, so he thought.

Forever craving his parents love, Mason would act out and cause trouble, even to the point where in some incidents the cops had been involved.

Kim and Dave always figured it was just teenage angst and would constantly make excuses for him in the hope that at some point, he would grow out of it. Unfortunately this was not meant to be and their parents passing only seemed to magnify his behaviour.

There had always been a rivalry between the brothers and so their parents had left everything to both of them equally in their will, to try and in hope that they would eventually work to together.

It wasn't until the reading of said will that they found out about the clause in it for Max. Needless to say that Mason was ecstatic about it, and gloated that their parents had loved him more than Max after all, because part of the clause was that if Max didn't get married by his thirty fifth birthday, then everything would go to Mason.

Mason had done everything in his power to stop Max from marrying anyone.

Max had been engaged once to Bethany, but Mason fixed that. He had lured Bethany to the cave where he had taken Izzy. He locked her in and left her there to die. When he went back six weeks later, he had buried her remains at the back of the cave, and then covered the grave with rocks.

Max had been in a right state over his missing fiancée. There had been a search party out looking for her. Her family had heard nothing from her either and sadly she was never found. That was six years ago and it had taken him a long time to come to terms that Bethany was never coming back. There had been other women, but Mason had managed quite easily to either scare them away or seduce them. On a couple of occasions, he had timed it so that Max would walk in on them while they were having sex.

Izzy was a different kettle of fish all together. She wasn't easily scared, she had stood up to him at the cave and she wouldn't, couldn't be seduced either.

A plan of action was needed and it needed to hit her where it hurt.

Who is the closest to her? Her family, but geography scuppered that plan.

Her best friend Lorna. Perfect.

The added bonus was that Lorna was seeing Max's friend Nick, so he could kill two birds with one stone. LITERALLY! He hatched a plan and waited for the right moment, but never imagined it would come sooner than expected.

CHAPTER THIRTY-TWO

Izzy and Lorna stood by the burned out ruins of the cottage. Lorna wiped an escaping tear from her cheek.

'Hey honey, it will be ok I promise. You will get through this' Izzy place a comforting arm around Lorna's shoulder 'I've been thinking…..maybe we should leave, go back home I mean'.

Lorna spun round. 'We can't leave now. Besides, the police may want to talk to us again and then there is Nick's funeral. Izzy I can't not go to that' she turned away and began sobbing again.

'Ok, we will stay until after the funeral. I'll see if Max has heard anything from Nick's family. If his body has been released yet'.

'Thanks Izzy, you're such a good friend. I don't know what I would have done without you'.

'Hey that's what best friends are for. Come on, let's get back to the house and get something to eat, I'm starved and I can ask Max about the funeral'.

Lorna nodded and linking arms they slowly strolled back to the house.

Max paced his study. Nick had to be somewhere; he only wished he could figure out where that was. The private detective he had hired hadn't got anywhere either, looking under every rock, every stone unturned. But where would Nick go? He could hardly ask his family, they still thought he was dead and was grieving. No, this was one puzzle he had to figure out by himself.

He went over to the window and looked out towards the burnt out cottage. In the distance he saw Izzy and Lorna walking up the dirt track. He sighed heavily. How was he going to convince Izzy that he loved her, that he was in love with her? She hated him right now, he knew that much. Then a thought occurred to him, like a giant light bulb had lit up above his head....... He would tell her the truth about Nick. She would then see that he trusted her whole heartedly and prove to her he loved her for real and just because of some stupid conditions in his fathers will.

CHAPTER THIRTY-THREE

Izzy and Lorna were sat at the kitchen table eating pasta that Izzy had made for them both. Lorna pushed it around her plate with her fork.

'Lorna honey, you have to try and eat something. You're turning in to a skeleton with skin on for gods sakes! Now eat, please'.

Lorna saw the pleading look on her friends face and nodded slowly before stabbing at a pasta twirl and putting it in to her mouth.

The kitchen door swung open and they both looked round to see Max entering.

'Hi' he said.

'Hi Max. Can I get you coffee?' Izzy asked.

'Thanks that would be great Izzy'.

Lorna watched the awkwardness between them and frowned. She figured they were trying not to flaunt their attraction to each other in front of her because of Nick and what they had had.

Izzy passed Max a cup of coffee. 'There you go, strong and nice and hot' she planted a fake smile and it didn't go unnoticed by Lorna.

'Thank you Izzy, just how I like it' Max said.

Lorna snapped, slamming her fork down on the table, she stood up.

'Whatever the hell is going on with you too, I don't care ok. You don't have to hide how you feel about each other because of what has happened to Nick. So stop all the awkward chit chat and kiss already, because it is that that is making me uncomfortable'. She pushed her chair back and then stormed out of the room.

Max and Izzy stood staring at the now closed kitchen door Lorna had just walked through and slammed for good measure.

After what seemed an age stood in silence, Max was the first to talk.

'Well that told us didn't it!' He turned slowly to face Izzy.

'Look Max I …. I, there's something I need to ask you. It's about Nick …' Max put his hand up, stopping her in her tracks.

'Yes I need to talk to you about Nick too, but it's not what you think'.

Izzy looked a little perplexed 'what do you mean Max?'

'We can't talk here. Can we go for walk, because what I have to say Lorna can't hear'.

She nodded and followed him out of the back door.

They had walked for quite a while and had headed up by the lake. Izzy stopped walking and turned to Max.

'Ok so we haven't said a word since we left the house. Talk Max and it better be good because if you have made all this up to just get me here ...' she spread her hands 'so you can try and persuade me again about how much you love me, then I'm going back to the house'.

'I haven't made anything up and there's no easy way to say it but....'.

'Oh for fucks sake Max, spit it out!'

Max sighed heavily and looked up at the sky.

'It's Nick...'

'What the fact he's dead?'

'If you let me finish I will tell you ...' he took a deep breath 'he's still alive, Nick is still alive. The man in the fire was my brother Mason'.

Izzy's hand went straight to her mouth to stifle the gasp. Her mind was racing. How could this be true? How could Nick be alive? Wouldn't he have been here if he was? Why wasn't he here? So many questions and they were frying her brain.

She sat down on the grassy verge and cupped her knees. Max sat down beside her.

'I know what you're thinking. All those questions running around in your head. Why, how and where is he now. Why hasn't he come back? What was Mason doing at the cottage? I know because I have been asking the same questions'.

Izzy turned to him 'why are you telling me all this?'.

'Because I trust you. Because your friend had a relationship with him'.

Izzy lay her head on his shoulder. 'Thank you'.

'For what?'.

'For trusting me. For loving me. For being honest with me …..
I'm sorry about before, about having a go at you, for accusing
you of using me'.

He wrapped his arm around her and taking hold of her hand,
he held it to his lips.

CHAPTER THIRTY-FOUR

Izzy's head spun round at the sound of rustling.

'What is that?' she whispered to Max.

'It's probably just a small animal. Nothing that can hurt you. Let's go back to the house and decide what we're going to do next' he looked up at the cloudy sky 'looks like a storm is coming, we had better hurry back...... should we tell Lorna about Nick. After our talk I am thinking that lying to her will bite us on the ass. What do you think, she's your friend, you know her better than anyone, how do you think she will take it?'

Izzy stood up and stretched 'I think we should tell her the truth. She doesn't deserve how he's treated her and I won't add to her misery. At least she can get over him and move on'.

A twig snapped in the distance. Izzy shrieked. Max grabbed her hand.

'Your safe with me' he reassured her.

She smiled at him as he pulled her in to his and kissed her forehead.

They walked back to the house hand in hand.

Mason stepped out from behind the large tree by the lake and chuckled to himself. His plan was in place and working. They didn't have a clue about anything.

With Nick out of the way, his next victim was going to be Lorna. He would lure her to the cave pretending to be Nick and do to her what he did to Max's first fiancée.

He would get rid of Izzy one way or another. She would either head back to England with Lorna's body in tow or if she decided to stay with Max, his plan would be to make her think her dead friend was haunting her.

He had to be quick though with his plan because Max's 35th birthday was fast approaching. He couldn't risk his brother marrying Izzy, not now. Not after all his hard work.

He would have to act tonight before it was too late.

CHAPTER THIRTY-FIVE

Lorna couldn't sleep. She had felt restless since getting in to bed. She had tried to read, usually that works. But not tonight. She lay there a few more minutes before slinging the cover back and getting out of the bed.

She grabbed her robe and put it on as she walked across the room to the window. The temperature had dropped and there was a slight chill in the air. She shivered and wrapped the robe tighter around her.

She could just make out the burned ruins of the cottage from her window and was stunned to see a light flashing.

She knew it wasn't Max or Izzy because she had seen them come back to house earlier.

She also knew it couldn't be the police either, not at this time anyway.

Lorna, always the nosey, curious one, made her way down the dirt track towards the cottage.

She could still see the light flashing throughout the ruin.

She shivered. Was she making a mistake coming down here to investigate? Maybe she should have woke Max and Izzy up.

She stopped dead in her tracks. The light had stopped

flashing. She rubbed her eyes. Maybe she had been seeing things. She was tired so could her eyes have been playing tricks on her?

"HELLO. WHO'S IN THERE?" She called out in to the darkness, but no-one answered.

Her body shuddered as she took in her surroundings. The trees rustled loudly as the wind grabbed at the leaves. It was pitch black and she realised that yes, it had been a mistake to come out here by herself.

She turned quickly, she could just make out the light at the house and was about to set off running back, when something or someone grabbed her from behind. She was catapulted backwards by the throat and slammed to the floor. She was so scared she closed her eyes tightly as she tried to grab and scratch at her assailant and was rewarded with a punch to her face that knocked her unconscious.

Lorna woke up with a splitting headache. Disorientated she figured it was a hangover until she felt her face then saw the blood on her hand. Letting out little scream she scrambled to her feet, realising she was barefoot and standing in dirt. The little light that was streaming in to the room seemed to be coming from a large wooden door. Only she wasn't in a room. She was in cave.

Lorna rushed over to the door and started banging on it, screaming for help, eventually collapsing on the floor with exhaustion.

She sobbed. Who had done this to her? Why had they done this to her? How long were they going to keep her here? What did they want from her? Are they going to kill me? Have they gone after Max and Izzy at the house?

All these questions raced through her head. Her thoughts drifted to Nick then. Could it have something to do with his death? The cottage fire? .... She had to get out of here. She had to warn Max and Izzy.

CHAPTER THIRTY-SIX

Izzy came in to the kitchen scratching her head, taking in the aroma of freshly made coffee. Max was stood by the coffee machine two cups out.

"Good morning sleepy head' he said with a wry smile.

"Morning. Why didn't you wake me? It's almost 10'.

"You looked so peaceful and I know you haven't been sleeping very well' he handed her a coffee and leaned against the breakfast bar.

Izzy yawned then asked if he had seen Lorna morning.

'No, why?'

'I checked in on her before I came down and she wasn't there. Her bed hasn't been made and her clothes are still on the chair so assumed she had come down for breakfast. I'll go have a look on the porch' she turned to leave.

'She's not out there and there's nothing to suggest she's had breakfast either. Though ......' he seemed to drift off in thought.

'What?

'I'm not sure. The door was unlocked this morning and I am damn sure I locked it last night'.

Izzy face drained of colour. 'Nick!

'I don't think so, if he wanted to hurt us in any way, I think he would have done it last night'.

'Maybe, but that doesn't explain where Lorna is. What if he's taken her... or worse...of god what if he's killed her like he did your brother?' she was hysterical down. Max wrapped his arms around her. His lips brushed against her forehead.

'Look, I'm sure she's fine. Why don't you go back to the bedroom and lock the door while I'll check the rest of the house and the stables. It's possible she's gone to see the horses'.

Izzy nodded, she didn't need telling twice.

Max on the other hand knew something didn't feel right. He would check the cottage ruins too, Lorna may have wandered down there, though he didn't hold too much on to that theory either.

Izzy locked the bedroom door. She decided to shower and get dressed rather than sit about twiddling her thumbs until Max came back.

The hot water washed away the tears that stung her cheeks. She had a bad feeling about Lorna that she just couldn't shake. Max had said not to worry and tried to reassure her before he went in search of Lorna and to secure the house and grounds. It still didn't make her feel any better though. She was restless now. She needed to go and look for her best friend.

She turned the shower off and was startled by loud banging and shouting on the bedroom door.

'Izzy are you ok. Answer me damn it. Open the door'.

It was Max. With a relieved sigh she rushed across the room and unlocked the door.

Max charged in and grabbed her by the arms. He looked like a mad man. His face softened when he saw the fear in her eyes.

'Izzy, I'm sorry. I didn't mean to scare you. I couldn't get in and you didn't answer me, I was scared something had happened to you. Please forgive me'. He pulled her close and held her tight.

She was almost scared to ask but she had to know. 'Max, did you find Lorna'?

Max sighed deeply against her temple. 'No, I'm sorry Izzy but she's no-where to be seen. I think we need to call the cops and I think we need to tell them everything about Nick and about Mason too'. Izzy whimpered and he held her even tighter.

CHAPTER THIRTY-SEVEN

Mason pulled the ski mask over his face. He didn't want Lorna to see it was him, at least not yet anyway.

Gripping tightly on to the crop he had taken from the stables earlier, he slowly unlocked the padlock and opened the large wooden door, standing back in case she lunged at him.

He needn't have worried. Shining his torch in to the darkness, he found her slumped against the wall, her eyes closed.

Fuck! She better not be dead. Maybe he had hit her harder than he thought. He was so looking forward to having some fun with her too.

Edging closer to her, he shone the torch in her face, then trailed the light down to her chest and watched with bated breath…………. With a relieved gasp, he saw her chest rise then fall. She is breathing, she is alive.

He kicked her foot with his hard heavy boot. Making her wince in pain as she opened her eyes.

She tried to focus her eyes to the blinding light that engulfed her face.

'STAND UP' the male voice bellowed at her. Using the cave wall as support, she scrambled to her feet. She would do as the man said for now, because she didn't want to die right at this moment. If he was going to kill her, she figured he would have done it by now and not kept her prisoner in this shit hole.

'CLOSE YOUR EYES AND TURN AROUND'.

Again she did as she was told. She felt his hands brush against her neck. She shuddered. The feel of his cold hands touching her skin made her feel sick.

He tied what felt like a scarf around her head, covering her eyes as a blindfold.

He grabbed her hands then, pulling them behind her back and tying her wrists tightly together with his neck tie. So tight in fact it made her squeal out in pain. But he didn't care.

Putting his mouth close to her ear, he sniggered.

'Perfect' he whispered.

'Please don't hurt me, I'll do anything you want. What do you want? Please let me go' she begged, but Mason just laughed at her.

'Yes Lorna, you will do anything I want'.

Who was this man? How did he know her name?

For a split second Lorna thought she recognised his voice, but couldn't place it. Could it be someone she knew? But who? She didn't know anyone here, other than Max, Nick and Mason. She knew it couldn't be Max because he was with Izzy and she had only met Mason once, it couldn't possibly be him and it definitely wasn't Nick because he was dead.

The only conclusion she could come up with was that he was some kind of mad maniac who had been lurking in the shadows, waiting. But then how did he even know her name and why would his voice sound familiar. She was confused, which was the understatement of the year.

It had to be someone she knew. The only way to find out would be to keep quiet and do whatever he wanted. The more he spoke would help her to figure out who it was.

'Lie down on your front' he ordered.

She lay down on the floor and waited for what was to come.

'Good girl. Now I don't want you to make a sound, do you hear me?'

Lorna nodded.

'Because if you do, you will get this...' he whipped her ass with the crop.

Lorna bit down on her lip so hard, she got the tin taste on her tongue from the blood that seeped out of the bite wound.

'Good. Now let us begin'.

Mason knelt down beside her. Using the crop, he ran it up her inner thigh, pulling her nightgown up and exposing her nakedness beneath.

'You are beautiful Lorna. Your skin is so soft. I may have to devour you'.

Holy fuck! She thought. As recognition hit her like a ton of bricks. This man. I know who it is.

MASON!

CHAPTER THIRTY-EIGHT

Izzy paced back and forth by the sitting room window. Her hands sore from the constant wringing. Max had gone to answer the door to the cops. She knew ringing them was the right thing to do, but she feared for her friend's safety.
What if calling them would put Lorna in more danger? Was that even possible? She could be dead already!
She was startled when the door swung open.
Max walked in followed by two police officers.
The first one looked about in his twenty's, slim build with short fair hair and piercing blue eyes. She reckoned he was about six feet tall. The second officer was older, probably in his sixty's. He was a short portly man with a receding hairline. He also seemed a little too jolly when he entered the room, which put Izzy instantly uneasy.
Max spoke first.
'Izzy, this is officer Zeke and officer Deacon'.
The older officer pushed forward with his hand held out.
'Pleased to meet you Miss Cruz. Anything we can do to help, that's what we are here for'.
'Oh, thank you officer Zeke, I really appreciate it'.
The younger officer stepped forward and shook Izzy hand.
'Miss Cruz. Mr Veto told us what has happened but if we

could get your version of things, that would be appreciated'.
Izzy nodded and sat down on the sofa.
She told them everything she could remember and about
how fearful she was for her friend Lorna.
Both officers stood by the fireplace nodding. Max had sat
down beside her and held her hand in support, giving it a
little squeeze of reassurance and encouragement when her
voice faulted.
Officer Deacon told officer Zeke to take a look around the
house and the grounds for any evidence. Deacon seemed to
be the one in charge Izzy figured. A little young for such a big
responsibility, but who was she to judge.

Izzy and Max were in the kitchen making coffee. Officer
Deacon had joined Zeke outside to cover more ground.
Both officers now headed in to the kitchen.
'We found what looks to have been some kind of scuffle
down by the burned out cottage. Is it possible your friend
went down there last night and why?' Deacon stared at Izzy,
making her feel like she was guilty of something.
'What? No I don't know why. Well ….'
'Yes Miss Cruz. What is it?'
'Well, since the fire, I have found her down there a few
times. I find it pretty creepy, but I think she needed to feel
close to Nick'.
'You mean the Nick that you believe to be still alive?'
'Look officer Deacon, we have both told you everything we
know. Izzy is scared for her friend Lorna; she is no-where in

the house or grounds. May I suggest you look further afield. She could be anywhere by now and the longer you are here asking us the same questions over and over the less chance you have of finding her'. Max had come to Izzy's side and wrapped his arm around her waist.

'Mr Veto. I am sure you are aware that the body recovered from the fire was examined. Blood tests, finger prints and the such. So I can assure you and reassure you that all forensic testing has concluded to the only possible outcome which is, that the body was Nick Elliot'.

CHAPTER THIRTY-NINE

Both Max and Izzy gasped with horror. Nick was really dead. That means that Mason is still alive. How could they have been so wrong about everything? And where the hell was Mason?

Izzy had to sit down before she collapsed. Max went to the sink and poured her a glass of water.

'I'm sorry Miss Cruz. It appears I have caused you extreme distress. Please accept my apologies'.

She put her head between her knees. How could this be happening? What did it mean?

She sat up with a start. 'Does this mean that Mason has Lorna?' she looked at Max. her eyes like a scared rabbit in a headlight.

Max handed her the water. 'I don't know sweetheart. Here drink this, it will make you feel better'.

Izzy jumped up, swiping the glass and knocking it across the room. Scattering glass and water everywhere.

'Are you fucking kidding me! Your brother has kidnapped my friend and doing god knows to her and you think drinking water is going to make me feel better! Fuck you Max. This is all your fault with your stupid will conditions. Having to get married so your knob head of a brother doesn't get everything. I wish I had never come here, I wish I had never met you, because Lorna would be safe and not locked away somewhere scared for her life. I hate you. Do you hear me? I hate you!' She stormed off and ran up to her bedroom, slamming the door and flinging herself on to bed.

'I am so sorry officers, I don't know what to say, I really don't. My brother is …. How do you say…… needy? Determined I guess, to get what he wants'.
'What he wants? As in Lorna Regan? As in everything?'
       'What exactly did Miss Cruz mean by everything Mr Veto?'
Max threw his head back and blew out a deep breath.
'Everything means just that. My brother has only a forty percent share in the farm. Our parents left the majority to me, but for me to own the house, business and everything else with it, I have to marry. My parents little joke I guess and their way of saying they trust my brother Mason. I suppose I should be flattered they thought highly of me enough to give me majority share but not highly enough for me to keep them…… if I don't marry then my brother gets everything'.
'Ok, so what does any of this have to do with Miss Regan's disappearance? Was it her you was to marry? Is that why you think your brother could have taken her?' Deacon asked.
'I don't know and no, my intentions were….are not to marry Lorna……' he looked towards the door then back at Deacon 'my intentions are to marry Izzy. I guess that's not looking so good now' he grimaced.

'Yes, that as may be. You had better go and check on Miss Cruz. We will do a sweep of the surrounding grounds to your property before we leave. If we find anything we'll let you know'.

Max nodded his approval, then watched the officers leave via the French doors.

Max hadn't heard back from the officers after three hours, so assumed there was nothing untoward beyond his property. He needed to clear his head. Izzy had been so mad at him it had broken his heart. He understood her frustrations and hurt, but how was that his fault?

All he knew was he had to get through to her somehow. Make her see that what was happening wasn't his fault and that Mason was the one to blame for all this.

He took the stairs two by two and rushed to Izzy's bedroom door. He tapped lightly on it. No answer. He tried again but a little louder. Still no answer. Maybe she was asleep, he thought. After all that has happened he wasn't surprised that it had drained her of energy.

He knocked a little louder this time and called through the door. 'Izzy, will you be ok? I'm going for a ride. I need to clear my head'.

She still didn't answer.

'Please answer me Izzy, so I know you are ok'.

He heard shuffling noises from inside and stood back from

the door. Izzy opened it. Her eyes blood shot and damp from crying.

'As you can see I am far from ok. But if it makes you feel any better, I will be fine. So you can go and have your ride. Now if you don't mind I'm exhausted and need to sleep'. She slowly closed the door on him.

It felt like Max had been riding for hours. He had stopped by the lake to let his horse take a drink.

The fresh air would do him good if nothing else.

At the opposite side of the lake was where his property ended. Glancing across he could just make out a vehicle parked up on the dirt track.

He knew there wasn't another property for miles, so who did that car belong to? Why was it parked there?

He grabbed the reins and mounted, trotting around the lake to the other side where the car was parked.

As he got closer, he realised it was a cop car. Must be Deacon and Zeke's patrol car. They must still be taking a look around.

He dismounted and tied the horses rein around a tree.

Walking around the car, he noticed one of the doors had been left open. Strange, he thought.

Max looked inside. The radio was off its hook and dangling on the floor. The gun holsters underneath the dash were empty. Fuck me! What did that mean? They had needed their guns for something..... for someone! Mason!

CHAPTER FORTY

Even after everything Mason had done, Max didn't want to see his brother dead. He had lost enough already.

Looking down the muck track he could see foot prints. He would follow them and try and stop Deacon and Zeke from harming his brother. Arrest him for what he has done yes, but not kill him.

Max mounted his horse and began following the trail.

'Come on boy, steady does it' he said to his horse, patting him in praise.

He had gone around fifty metres when he heard a noise coming from the ditch by the side of the track. Max stopped, dismounted and slowly edged towards where he could hear the noise coming from. It was more of a groan, like someone was in pain.

The ditch was slightly covered with shrubbery and he couldn't see anything at first. He brushed away a dense part of it and saw a leg, partially bare from the ankle. A black sock, no shoe. The bottom of the trousers was ripped.

Max called out. 'HELLO, CAN YOU HEAR ME?'

He heard another groan.

Max leapt in to action. He jumped down in to the ditch and landed right in a muddy pool of water. He cursed but when he looked up he was shocked to see who it was laying in front of him.

'Deacon! Shit what happened? Where's Zeke? Where are you hurt? Here …. Grab my hand'.

Deacon lifted his right arm and grabbed hold of Max's hand. As Max pulled he could see that Deacons left arm was injured. Blood running down from a wound on his shoulder.

'You've been shot' Max observed as he helped Deacon up the slope and on to level ground.

'Fuck. Have you found Zeke?' Deacon asked.

'What? No I haven't seen him. What happened? Was this Mason's doing?'

'We need to find Zeke, then I'll tell you what happened'. Deacon checked his gun was still in his hip holster, taking it out he checked how much ammo he had left. He then headed off, limping back up the dirt track.

'Hey wait for me' Max hurried to catch up with him.

Max realised they were ending towards the quarry. He hadn't been up there since him and his brother were kids. They spent most of their summer there, swimming and playing in the caves nearby.

'Deacon, are you going to tell me what the hell happened to you or am I just to guess?'

Deacon gave him a sideways glance 'fine. I will tell you, but when we get up there I want you to hang back ok. I mean it Mr Veto. Your brother is a dangerous man and I am damned if I'm going to have your death on my conscience'.

'I hear what you're saying, but my brother wouldn't hurt me. Whatever he's done I know that much'.

Deacon stopped dead and turned to Max.

'Mr Veto, in case you forgot, your brother killed Nick Elliot then set fire to the cottage to cover it up. He also tried to make out it was him that had died and for all we know he may have Miss Regan held captive somewhere. That is if he hasn't killed her yet and on top of that he has attempted to kill a police office, ME! God knows what he has done to officer Zeke, because we got separated in the commotion. All I know is we have to find Zeke and your brother. I was attempting to call for back up when your brother jumped me. We fought and in my attempt to give chase, he shot me and I rolled down the embankment. I don't know what happened to Zeke after your brother hit him over the head with the butt of the gun. I assumed he had come to and went after your brother. I guess I was wrong' Deacon hung his head in shame. He should have been able to take Mason down then Zeke would be here now.

It was a lot for Max to take in. if what he said was true, then Nick was already dead before the fire was started.

'How did Nick die?'

'What?' Deacon looked up.

'I asked you how Nick died. You said he was already dead before the fire was started'.

'Well the evidence suggested he was knocked unconscious then strangled with bare hands. I must say it takes a special kind of coward to do that to another human being. Anyway enough of this chit chat, we need to find Zeke and your brother'.

They reached a clearing where you can see the side of the caves started and just beyond that was the quarry.
'Stay here while I take a look around'.
Max heard something in the distance. A scream he thought.
'Wait. Look, it's Mason and he has Lorna. Deacon what do we do?'
'We don't do anything. Stay here'.
'If you think I'm going to stay here and twiddle my thumbs, think again. He has Lorna and brother or not, he isn't getting away'.
Deacon nodded. He really didn't have enough energy to deal with Mason and argue with Max too.
They crept slowly forward as they watched Mason dragging Lorna by the arm. They could see she was blind folded and her wrists were tied behind her back.
She screamed for him to let her go, which of course only made him more angry. He grabbed her hair and yanked her head back.
'Shut the fuck up or I will kill you right here right now'. He pulled her along, heading towards the quarry.
Max feared he was going to throw her in. He couldn't let that happen. He came out from around the rock him and Deacon had hidden behind and shouted at his brother.

'Mason. What the fuck are you doing man? This isn't you. Why don't you let Lorna go and we can talk about it'.

Mason's head whipped round. The shock of seeing his brother there almost knocked him off of his feet.

'What the fuck! Stay back Max, or she'll get it. I mean it. I will pop her in the head right now'.

Max backed off a little when he saw Mason had a gun held to Lorna's temple.

Deacon edged his way around the other side of the rock while Max kept Mason busy.

'Ok Mason, I'm backing off. At least tell me what all this is about. Why have you got Lorna tied up like that'.

'What I do is none of your business Max. You've never been interested in anything I have done before, so why start now. Lorna and me and have been getting to know each better. Haven't we Lorna' he tugged at her hair, pulling her neck back. She winced at the pain.

'I said haven't we Lorna' Mason said again through gritted teeth.

'Yes' she whimpered.

'Lorna, everything will be ok, I promise' Max tried to reassure her.

'Don't make promises you can't keep brother dear' Mason laughed gruffly.

'The one thing I always do. Brother dear! Is I always, always, keep my promises. I have no intention of going back on this one. That is a promise'.

'And just how do you intend to do that Max, after all. I am the one holding the gun. I suggest you...........'

'FREEZE! PUT THE GUN DOWN NOW AND GET TO YOUR KNEES' Deacon barked. He had managed to get around the other side so he was behind Mason.

'Very good Max. I didn't know you had it in you'. Mason dropped the gun on the floor and dropped to his knees.

Max rushed over to Lorna and walked her back to the rock. He removed her blindfold and untied her wrists. With her arms free, she flung them around Max's neck and held on tight, as if her life depended on it.

Behind them they heard a commotion. They looked round and saw officer Deacon on the floor and Mason running up towards the quarry.

Max shouted after him to stop, but Mason kept on going.

'Wait here and check on Deacon. I'm going after Mason'.

'Max wait. He's dangerous, he'll kill you' she grabbed his arm and wouldn't let go.

'I'll be ok, I promise and you know I always keep my promises. Izzy will be relieved to see you, she's been so worried about you. Now see to Deacon, try and get him back to the patrol car. Here's my phone, when you get a signal call the police and tell them what's happened and where we are, ok'.

Lorna nodded. She watched him get further and further away as Max raced after Mason. Would she ever see him again? If

Mason killed him then he would come back and finish Deacon off and kill her too. She had to get back to the car.

CHAPTER FORTY-ONE

Lorna hobbled over to Deacon. She checked his pulse. He was alive but barely. No way would she get him to the car on her own. Her only option was to leave him there. The cops and paramedics will see to him when they get there.

She hobbled back to the rock and looked over her shoulder. The coast was clear.

At the car she managed to get the radio working and told the dispatcher everything but was told it would be thirty minutes before anyone could get to her and for her to stay where she was.

How could she though? How could she stay put, knowing Max was with Mason. Izzy would never forgive her if she didn't even try and help. But what could she do? She was battered and bruised all over and in pain. Surely Izzy would understand if she was to stay put, like she was told to do. Her best friend wouldn't want her hurt any more than she already was.

Max could and would deal with Mason.

Shots rang out, echoing across the silent wilderness.
Startled, Lorna got in to the car and locked the doors. She
looked for keys but there weren't any. Shit! Officer Deacon
must have them. No way was she going back up there. What
if Mason has shot Max and is on his way to her now?
Lorna couldn't breathe. Panic rose up in to her throat and she
let out a strangled scream. Gripping tightly on to the steering
wheel, she tried to control her breathing and gain some sort
of control. Unfortunately, the same couldn't be said for Max!

CHAPTER FORTY-TWO

Max reached the top of the quarry where he found Mason with his back to him, stood at the very edge.

'MASON! Max called out, panting and trying to catch his breath, his brother turned to face him.

'Don't come any closer Max' he looked down in to the depths of the watery quarry. His footing slipped a little and dislodged the rubble that cascaded over the edge.

'Please Mason, just come back away from the edge' the panic in his voice made Mason laugh so loudly, it echoed.

'My brother, the wise one. Do you really think I am going to jump to a watery death when I have this' Mason held up the gun and pointed it at Max.

'For fuck sake Mason. Put the gun down. What the hell do you think I'm going to do?'

'Don't patronize me Max. do you really think I am that stupid? I'll tell you what's going to happen. You my dear brother, are going to turn around and go back down the ridge, so I can make my escape'.

'That isn't going to happen Mason. After what you've done, you're going to prison'.

Mason's smile left him now. If only Max knew the half of it. Maybe he should tell him, after all what did he have to lose now.

'I suppose you had better add Bethany to that long list of "things" I have done'. He goaded Max.

'What the hell is that supposed to mean? Did you have sex with ... with ...' Max couldn't bring himself to say it.

'Let's just say I enjoyed every inch of her before she left this mortal coil'.

Max clenched his fists. Had Mason killed Bethany all those years ago? He had to be lying, but then he hadn't heard anything from her and assumed she didn't want to be found. **'What did you do to her Mason'** Max said through gritted teeth, taking a step forward **'tell me now. I want to know everything'.**

'She's dead Max. That's all you need to know. Now step back and let me go'.

Max wasn't going to let him get away. He needed to know what he did to his fiancé Bethany.

He took another step forward.

'Fine I'll tell you, but step back or I will shoot you and then you'll never find out what happened to her'.

Max nodded and took two steps back.

'Remember the day of the family picnic?'

Max nodded.

'I lured her away, telling her you had said to meet you at the cave. I locked her in then went back later that night. She was like a feral cat and almost scratched my eyes out. Of course I had to punish her for that.

'Anyway, I played with her for a few days until I got bored. She was a handful and I was getting tired of reining her in. I get why you wanted to marry her though, she was….. how do you say ….. ahh yes, delectable. Enough was enough though so I locked her in and left her there. I went back after about four months, I knew she should be dead by then with having no food or water'.

Max fell to his knees. His voice caught in his throat, the words came out croaky 'How could you do such a thing?'

'Easy. I just threw her in there' he motioned to the muddy depths of the quarry.

'Why Mason? Why would you do that? All this?'

'Because I want it all Max. You have everything and I have nothing. I hated mum and dad for that and I knew if you got married then I would be left with nothing'.

Anger overflowed within Max and he lunged at Mason.

Mason tried to aim the gun at Max and fired it, but the bullet flew passed, missing Max by a hair and hitting the tree behind him.

With Max's arms wrapped around Mason's waist, they both fell over the edge and in to the dark murky depths.

CHAPTER FORTY-THREE

Max crawled up the mud sodden embankment. His hands sinking in to the clay, as he dragged himself out of the water. He rolled on to his back and looked up at the now darkening sky.

His thoughts drifted to Izzy. She would be worried. Regardless how angry she was at him, she would still be worried about him and about Lorna.

He pushed himself up to a sitting position and looked out across the vast watery grave that had consumed Mason.

He had tried to save his brother. Had tried to grab him as they sunk beneath the depths, but the blackness before his eyes made him blind to see anything in front of him.

He had come up for air a few times and dived back down, but it was no use. He had to give up or die too.

Hearing a noise from above, Max looked up and was relieved to see a Police chopper. Back up had arrived, if a little too late.

Max lay back down and waited. He sighed heavily, feeling reassured that he would be found and back in the arms of Izzy. Now that Lorna had been found safe and well. Yes she was battered and bruised and her mental state will need a close eye kept on, but she was alive, that was the main thing.

He closed his eyes and drifted off in to a deep sleep. His body was exhausted. His brain was exhausted. Hell! Everything was exhausted.

Izzy held his hand. When she saw Max laid in the hospital bed on a drip, she had gasped in horror. She told him over and over she was sorry, but he wouldn't hear her apologies because he was still unconscious.
The police searchers had found him by the quarry embankment. There had been no sign of Mason or even a body for that matter.
They told her not to worry, when she had begun to shake and saw the fear in her eyes. That there was no way he could have survived.
Izzy wasn't convinced though. If Max had managed to get out then Mason could have too.
Right now though she could only think about Max.

Max stirred. His eyes opening slowly and taking in his surroundings as they focused on the person sat next to his bed.
Izzy was sleeping, her hand still covering his. Max released his hand and placed it on top of hers, giving it a squeeze.
He couldn't believe she was here, here with him.
She opened her eyes wide and jumped up, kicking the chair over.

'Max you're awake! I thought I had lost you. When the police called to say both you and Lorna were in the hospital…. I ….'. Her voice left her.

'It's ok. I'm ok. How is Lorna?'

'She's fine. A little bruised but apart from that she's ok. I can't believe you found her. I can't tell you how grateful I am. I don't know what I would have done if anything had happened to her ……or to you.

'I'm sorry about what I said before. I don't hate you and I know what happened to Lorna had nothing to do with you'. Max placed a finger to her lips 'It's ok Izzy. Let's forget about all that now and move on. There is something I need to talk to you about though, but not here. When we get home. We can talk properly then, ok?'

Izzy nodded. She moved closer and lay her head on his chest. His heart beating against her cheek, strangely gave her comfort.

CHAPTER FORTY-FOUR

Lorna watched her friend pace back and forth and laughed at her, making her stop.

'What?'

'Izzy if you don't keep still, you're going to make an indentation in the bedroom carpet'.

Izzy looked down at the floor 'sorry' then came and sat down next to Lorna on the bed.

'Lorna, what do you think he wants to talk about? I mean he's asked me to dress up "nice" and when I looked in the dining room the table was set for a candlelight dinner.

'What do you think that means?'

'Dear god Izzy, you can be a bit thick sometimes'.

Izzy gave her friend a sideways glance and a grimace.

'Well I don't know do I'.

'Izzy for fucks sake. The man is going to ask you to marry him'.

Shocked, Izzy stood up and face Lorna. 'Don't be ridiculous. He doesn't have to marry anyone anymore. Not now that Mason is...... well you know'.

'I don't think he's asking you because of that sweetheart. I think he's asking you because he loves you and he really does want you to be his wife.

'You'd be stupid not to accept. You do love him back don't you?'

Izzy walked over to the window and watched the dusk disappear in to the night.

Did she love him? Really love him though, enough to give everything up in England for? Everything? What on earth was she on about! She didn't have anything to give up in England. What would her life here be like though? She would be set for life. No money worries. Anything she wanted, she could have. The best thing about it though would be Max. She would be his wife. A man who loved her to the moon and back and she loved him just as much. What more could she asked for ……..nothing.

She entered the dining room. Max was standing by the table pouring wine in to two glasses. He looked when he heard the door open and gasped as his heart skipped, the butterflies in his tummy were doing somersaults. The outpour of love he felt for her was beyond anything he had ever felt for anyone before.

'You look beautiful Izabella Cruz. Please come, take a seat' he pulled out a chair for her.

'What's with full naming me?' she asked, as she sat down.

Max laughed and took the seat beside her. Taking the napkin out the holder, he placed it on his lap. Izzy followed suit.

'Sorry, I didn't mean any offence. I think you have a beautiful name just like the woman it belongs to'.

Izzy gave him a wry smile. 'Corny, but thanks anyway'.

Max chuckled and picked up his wine glass 'A toast is in order'.

Izzy picked hers up 'To what?'

'To us. To being here. To being alive and well. Cheers'.

They clanked glasses and took a sip.

'I hope you're hungry. I feel I may have cooked far too much' he said, taking another sip of wine.

'I could call Lorna down. She's always hungry, she would love this …..' she looked at the dishes with suspicion '….this… sorry … what is it?'

Max almost spat his wine out as he bellowed with laughter.

'What?' she giggled.

'Do you know how much I love you Izzy? Because in case you didn't, I would die for you. In fact I almost did.

'Marry me Izzy. I would be lost without you. After everything we have been through, I never thought I would ever feel like this about anyone ever again. I know we haven't known each other very long, but when you crashed in to my life, it was like I had been hit in the heart with a love meteor. My life hasn't been the same since……. please say yes. Be my wife, so I can show you every day how much you mean to me'.

Izzy didn't know what to say. She had half expected what he was going to say after what Lorna had said to her in the bedroom earlier. It was still a shock though.

'Please say something Izzy. Don't leave me hanging here'.
She looked up at him, searching his face. Taking hold of his hand in both hers, she held it to her heart.
'Max, do you feel that? That is the heart beat of a woman in love. I would like nothing more than to be your wife, so yes, I will marry you'.
Max leaned across and kissed her softly.
'This is our new beginning Izzy'.

THREE MONTHS LATER

Lorna stood behind Izzy who was sat at the dressing table.
She looked at her friends reflection in the mirror.
'You look so beautiful Izzy. I think I might cry'.
'Stop it or you'll set me off again and I don't want to ruin my
make-up' Izzy laughed.
Lorna squeezed her friends shoulders 'are you ready for the
veil?'
Izzy nodded.
Lorna crossed the bedroom and picked up the veil that rested
on the bed.
She positioned it on Izzy's head and fastened it in with
hairpins. She spread it out over her shoulders and stood back
to allow Izzy to stand up.
'Are you ready to take a look?'
'Yes'.
Lorna turned the full length mirror round.
Izzy's hands went straight to her face. 'OH GOSH!' she
gasped.
'I KNOW! I told you didn't I, just how beautiful you looked'.
She checked her watch. It was ten past two. Ten minutes late
but that was ok. After all it was tradition that the bride is
always late.

'Right then, time to go. I think we've kept the groom waiting for long enough' Lorna said.
'Ok here we go'.

The ceremony went without a hitch, thank goodness.
They had feared a couple of months back that it might not even happen. Max's solicitors had called him in and said they needed to "talk to him about the will".
They needn't have worried. There had been another clause in the will that neither Max or Mason knew about. It stated that if either one of them died, then the everything would automatically go to the other. Meaning that the marriage clause would become null and void.

In the last three months. Lorna had attended Nick's funeral.
She also helped Izzy with the wedding arrangements.
The police had closed the case file on Mason and declared him dead. Much to Max's chagrin, who had hoped his brother had gone to prison for his crimes. Death was the easy way out.
Deacon recovered from being shot in the shoulder and the stomach. Zeke wasn't so lucky. He had been found bludgeoned to death inside the cave.
Now he concentrated on making a life with Izzy. Maybe even start a family. They had laid in bed one night and talked about their future. About how many children they would

have. Two boys and two girls and what they would call them. They talked about expanding the business and for Izzy to take more of a role in helping run it.

They had their future planned out and thankfully there was no-one and nothing now to stop that happening.

CHAPTER FORTY-FIVE

Izzy flopped on to the bed. Exhausted was the understatement of the year. It had been a fantastic and very long day.

Lorna had taken a fancy to one of Max's distant cousins and disappeared off somewhere. Only later to be seen coming from the direction of the stables, hair and clothes at disarray with said cousin following behind her. Equally dishevelled. Izzy had shaken her head at her. She was just happy that her friend was back to herself.

Izzy had feared for Lorna's sanity after everything that had happened, but she hadn't needed to worry. Lorna was back to her usual happy go lucky, live in the moment self. Which in turn made Izzy happy.

'Hey you, Mrs Veto or should I be saying Mrs daydreamer?' Max said, as he stood by the bed unbuttoning his shirt.

Izzy sat up 'sorry, I was just thinking about how happy Lorna is. How she's bounced back.......' she knelt up on the bed and slipped her arms around his neck '.... now though I am thinking about what I am going to do to you'.

Max wrapped his arms around her waist and pulled her close to him.

'Well I'm thinking about what I am going to do to **you,** my darling wife'.

They made love. At first with a heat so passionate they couldn't breathe. They had laid catching their breath for a while before cuddling. Then had made love again. Slower, more softly the second time. Coming together, they had looked deeply in to each other's eyes and then holding each other, had fallen in to a deep sleep.

CHAPTER FORTY-SIX

Max awoke with a start. The loud bang had brought him out of a deep sleep.

He looked over at Izzy. Good, the noise hadn't disturbed her. He crept out of bed and tip toed to where his robe was draped over the chair.

Fastening the belt tightly, he quietly opened the bedroom door and made his way down the stairs.

Half way down he heard the bang again. It sounded like someone hitting a hard surface with a hard object.

As Max reached the bottom of the stairs, he picked up one of the heavy candlesticks from the console table and headed towards where the noise was coming from.

He stopped outside his study and pressed his ear to the door. The banging was coming from inside.

Max grabbed the handle and tentatively turned it, opening the door he stood frozen to the spot.

'Hello brother dear. You certainly took your time.

Congratulations by the way. I see you married the delectable and divine Izabella Cruz after all.

I must say, she does have the most sexy body I have ever seen. In fact, I would go as far as to say that she's sexier than …. oh what was her name? You know the one Max …. ahh yes

Bethany wasn't it? Yes, that's right'.

'Not one more fucking word Mason' Max couldn't hold in his anger. He lunged forward. Diving across the desk, he grabbed Mason around the throat. Both falling to the ground, they struggled. Throwing punches, trying to make contact. The adrenalin pumping through both of their body's.

Max caught Mason a heavy blow to the side of his head, then managed to drag himself up to his feet and stood back, gasping for breath.

'Get up you piece of shit. Do you hear me. I said get up Mason'.

Holding the side of his head, Mason pulled himself up off of the floor.

They both turned their heads when they heard a sound by the door.

'MAX, LOOK OUT!' Izzy cried out.

Max turned just in time to see Mason charging towards him.

CHAPTER FORTY-SEVEN

Izzy screamed as Mason rugby tackled Max to the floor. They grappled around while Izzy watched on in horror.

She hadn't noticed Lorna stood behind her until she heard a loud breathy gasp.

'Izzy do something'.

'Like what? What do I do' the desperation in her voice made Lorna act quickly. The last thing she wanted was for her friend to become a widow on the same day she had become a wife.

She pushed Izzy out of the way, which happened to be further in to the study. Scanning the room Lorna saw a lamp on the desk. She rushed over, grabbed the lamp and turned to see Mason on top of Max with his hands around his neck. Izzy was screaming for Mason to get off of him. Like that would help!

With one big swing, the lamp made contact with the back of Mason's head. He fell sideways and slumped to the floor.

'Is he dead?' asked Izzy.

'I don't know. Check on Max and I'll have a look'.

'Lorna be careful'.

Izzy knelt beside Max and brushed her hand over his cheek.

'Max'.

He reached up to his neck and caressed his throat, wincing at the pain.

His voice croaky 'that son of a bitch won't be happy until I'm dead'.

'Please try not to talk. I'll go and get you some iced water, it will help soothe your throat'. Izzy hurried out of the study.

Max managed to sit up and looked over at his brother. Lorna was knelt beside him checking his pulse.

'Is he dead?'

Lorna shook her head 'no, unfortunately the bastard is still alive. He just unconscious. I say we tie him up and call the police'.

Max was debating what to do. Now that his brother was alive the will was void when it came to everything belonging to Max. There had been nothing to suggest a clause was in effect if any of them went to prison. Their parents obviously thought better of Mason than Max ever did. So now what? He didn't have a clue.

Izzy returned with a glass of ice water and handed it to Max, who sipped it slowly.

Izzy motioned to Mason who was still laid on the floor.

Lorna shook her head 'he's unconscious, mores the pity!'

'We should ring the police' said Izzy.

'Yes we should, but I say we should have a little fun of our own with him. I want to see him tortured like he has done to us. To me. He would have killed me if Max hadn't come to the rescue. He would have thrown me in to the quarry and never looked back. I want him to suffer until he's begging us for mercy'. A smirk spread across Lorna's face as she spoke. Izzy couldn't believe what her friend was saying. The evilness that was coming out of Lorna's mouth made Izzy shiver in fear for her friends mentality.

'Lorna no! Don't say such things. If we did all these things to him just like he did to us. To you. Then we will be no better than him. We have to let the police deal with him. He will go to prison for a long time Lorna, for everything that he has done'.

Max stood between the two women. Watching. Listening. They both had a point.

CHAPTER FORTY-EIGHT

Max opted for tying his brother to a chair and calling the cops. There was no way he would or could stoop to Masons level.

Lorna had stormed off. She wasn't impressed with his choice, but Max didn't want to see her cross that line. Hell! Izzy would never have forgiven him if he had.

His brother needed to pay for his wrong doings regardless of how that would affect his inheritance.

He walked across the room and poured himself a whiskey. He motioned to Izzy if she wanted one pouring, but she shook her head and hugged herself.

She looked so scared. He hated that.

Izzy moved to the sofa and sat down. Max had lit the fire while they waited for the police to arrive.

'What do you think will happen to him Max' Izzy asked.

'I don't know. Probably held on remand until a trial date I guess. You're tired, come on I'll take you up. I'll wait for the cops to come'.

Izzy was hesitant 'wha….what about him' she nodded in Masons direction.

'He's not going anywhere. He will be unconscious for a while yet. Lorna hit him pretty hard you know, he's lucky to be alive. He's probably got concussion so I reckon he'll be taken to hospital for observation and kept under guard'.

Izzy nodded. Max wrapped his arm around her waist as he guided her upstairs.

They hadn't seen Lorna hiding around the corner at the bottom of the stairs.

She peered through the door of the study and saw Mason still tied to the chair, his head down, chin touching his chest.

Looking behind her to make sure no-one was there, she entered the room and closed the door.

In her right hand she held a large knife she had procured from the kitchen.

She stood in front of him, staring for a second before grabbing hold of his hair and yanking his head up. The action brought him round and it took him a while to focus on who was hurting him.

Lorna held the knife against his throat.

'DO IT BITCH' he sneered.

'Don't tempt me, because right now I could easily and happily slice your throat like butter. You're a monster and you deserve to die for what you did'.

'I'm not the one with a knife to someone's throat sweetheart. I think you'll find you are the monster, but then again I always thought that you and I are quite similar' he sniggered at her.

'I AM NOTHING LIKE YOU' she spat out at him and pressed the knife a little harder, slightly etching in to his skin. A smear of blood tarnished the edge of the blade.

She pulled his head back further exposing his neck. Lifting the knife, the point of it glistened in the fire light. Her hand coming down with force to plunge the knife in to him.

CHAPTER FORTY-NINE

'LORNA NO, STOP!' Max entered the room just in time to see her about to plunge the knife in to Mason.

Her hand haltering mid-air, she turned round to face Max.

'How can you say that after what he has done. He killed your fiancé among other things for fucks sake!' Lorna screeched.

'I know exactly what he did, I don't need reminding. Now give me the knife. The cops are on their way, let them deal with him'. He stepped forward, but Lorna put her hand up, stopping him in his tracks.

'I'm sorry Max, but I can't let him get away with what he's done' she raised the knife again.

Max rushed forward and grabbed the knife out of hand.

'The cops will be here any minute, do you really want to go down for killing that scum. Think of Izzy and what it would do to her if you went to prison. Is that what you want? Lorna think' he put his finger to her temple.

Lorna's shoulders slumped. She knew he was right. She couldn't do that to Izzy. She meant more to her than what killing him, meant to her.

Max and Lorna looked at each wide eyed as they heard sirens coming towards the house.

'Lorna go upstairs to Izzy now and stay there'.

'What are you going to do with the knife?'

'Lorna just do as I say, please'.

When she had gone, Max quickly went to his desk and put the knife in one of the draws.

Mason didn't say a word but watched Max's every move.

Max went over to the window and looked out. The cops were just pulling up, there sirens now soundless but the lights still flashing.

He faced Mason. Mason sniggered at him. Max could have and wanted to punch him right in that smarmy face of his. Instead he just shook his head at him and left the room to let the cops in.

'Hello Mr Veto, I believe your brother is alive and well and he's here. Where about in the house is he?'

'Please follow me, he's in the study. I'm afraid I had to tie him up so he couldn't escape again'.

But when they entered the room, Mason was gone.

'What the fuck!' Max exclaimed.

'I thought you said your brother was in here Mr Veto?'

'He was. The bastard has got free somehow. He can't have gotten far'.

The cop in charge told the other officers to search the house and grounds. There was no way he would have got too far from the property, if Mr Veto was correct when saying he was tied up when he had answered the door to them.

CHAPTER FIFTY

Max tapped on the bedroom door. Lorna answered it. Izzy
was sat on the bed when he entered.

'Are you two ok?' he asked.

'What's going on Max? What's happening?' asked Lorna.

'Mason got away.......he....' he stopped when he saw the
terror on Izzy's face. He rushed to her side and held her
close. 'Hey, it will be ok. The cops are here and they will find
him. He can't have got too far'.

Lorna paced the room '**I knew something like
would happen. Did you let him go Max? .....
well did you**?' she spat at him.

'No I did not, so stop the accusations. This isn't helping' he
snapped back.

She was about to say something then stopped when she saw
the pleading look on Izzy's face.

She came and sat at the other side of her.

'Izzy I'm sorry' she looked at Max then back at Izzy 'look, why
don't I go and make some tea for everyone?'

Max shook his head 'no-one is allowed to wonder the house
or grounds until Mason has been found'.

'This is ridiculous! Are we supposed to stay locked in up here for however long that is? I'm hungry now, I need to eat. Can I get you two anything while I'm down there?' enquired Lorna.

'Please Lorna. Just do what the police have asked' Izzy begged.

Lorna sighed and slumped down in the chair near the door and said 'Fine! I'll starve to death instead'.

Max stood up and went over to the window. Outside he could see the place was swarming with cops. Giving him some comfort in the knowledge that Mason was probably long gone by now and nowhere near the house, let alone inside. He figured it would be safe enough to go downstairs for something to eat. But not the girls. He would go and make them something, just to be on the safe side.

'Why don't I go make us all some food' he said, without turning around.

'Fine. I want bacon, eggs, fried bread, sausage and beans. Oh and a cup of tea' requested Lorna.

'What about you Izzy?' Max asked her.

'I don't think I can eat anything. I feel sick'.

Max nodded and headed towards the door. Lorna grabbed his arm. 'Be careful Max' she warned.

CHAPTER FIFTY-ONE

Max stood at the kitchen window looking out as he waited for the food to cook. He had turned on the coffee machine too. The least he could do was give the cops some sustenance while they searched for his brother.

Max had so many questions for his brother, like where had he been for the last few months? Why would he come back? As he pondered these questions his eyes drifted towards the stables. He could see someone moving about near the side. Just one of the cops, he dismissed.

He squinted to try and get a better look.

He began to tremble as anger emanated throughout his body when he realised what or who he was seeing. It was not one of the cops but Mason!

Damn him! He's like a bad smell.

Without giving it a second thought, he ran out of the back door and headed towards the stables.

As he rounded the corner he saw Mason crouched down by the far exit.

The only way Max would be able to get a hold of Mason was if he sneaked up behind him. He didn't want to make Mason aware of his presence.

Max crept slowly towards his brother, taking extra care not

to step on anything that would alert him to his approach. Unfortunately for Max, he hadn't taken the straw lined floor throughout the stables in to consideration.

The first couple of crunches under foot, he managed to get away with. The next step would be his undoing.

Mason quickly spun round. Eyes wide in shock. He began to run with Max following.

'MASON STOP!' Max called out but Mason wasn't stopping for no-one.

Running towards the wooded area, he hadn't noticed the two cops making their way back through towards the stables. They stopped when they heard Max shouting and hid behind the trees, waiting for Mason to come their way.

As Mason approached the trees, the two cops jumped out and pointed their guns at him.

'FREEZE. GET DOWN ON YOUR KNEES AND PUT YOUR HANDS BEHIND YOUR HEAD' they instructed.

Max came to a halt. An air of relief on his face when he saw the two cops cuffing Mason.

Back at the house, Max made his way up to the bedroom, back to the girls.

He tapped on the door and let them know it was him. Lorna opened the door.

Max went over to Izzy and grabbed her up in arms, holding her tight.

When he finally released her he spoke.

'The cops have got Mason. It's over'.

'Are you screwing with us?' said Lorna as she closed the door and sat down on the bed.

'No. They've caught him. I saw them handcuff and take him to the van. They want statements from us of course, but I told them tomorrow. I think we've been through enough after last night and this morning'.

Izzy nodded. She felt numb. She couldn't believe it was over. That her and Max could finally live their lives and Lorna too. A new beginning for them all ....finally.

EIGHT MONTHS LATER

Masons trial had been a short process, thank god! He had been found guilty without a shadow of a doubt by the jury. To be fair, Mason had accepted his wrong doings and had pleaded guilty to all charges.

As he stood in the dock now awaiting the judges sentencing, Max, Izzy and Lorna watched from the gallery.

They had all given evidence at the trial. Izzy had struggled though and it wasn't until she had fainted in the court room that she realised she was pregnant. At least something good has come out of this awful tragedy.

Max of course had been delighted and as for Lorna, well let's just say excited was an understatement. She had fussed on her friend ever since, which irritated Izzy to start with. She soon gave in though, because her best friend was just looking after her, after all.

The judge entered the court room and everyone stood up then sat down when asked everyone to be seated.

He wasted no time in passing his judgement and sentencing Mason.

'Would the prisoner stand please'.

Mason stood, flanked by two officers of the court. His lawyer also stood.

'Mason Veto. On the count of first degree murder, I sentence you to twenty five years.

On the count of second degree murder, I sentence you to fifteen years.

On the count of attempted murder, I sentence you to eight years.

On the count of attempted murder, I sentence you to eight years'.

There were gasps and loud whispering from the gallery.

Izzy's astonishment showed on her face as she turned to Max who squeezed her hand gently for reassurance. He knew she was thinking of him and how he was taking the news. Fifty-six years was a long time. Mason would be in his eighties when he would be released. That's if he didn't die in prison.

Lorna however, jumped up and whooped with excitement at the sentence.

'I hope you rot in jail you scumbag' she screamed, as the officers escorted Mason out of the court room.

He stopped for a second, looking directly at Lorna. His eyes bore in to hers. The look of horror on her face pleased him somewhat and he tipped his head, smirked and winked at her before being dragged away.

CHAPTER FIFTY-TWO

Izzy and Evie held hands as they spun round and around by the lake. The sunshine was glorious today, so Izzy had decided they would have a picnic by the lake while Max was in the city for a meeting.

Business was booming and they had expanded twice over the last seven years.

Feeling a little dizzy, they both collapsed on the ground giggling.

Izzy checked her watch. It was almost four thirty. Max had said he would be home by five.

'Shit! Come on Evie, we need to get back, daddy will be home soon and I need to get tea on'.

Gathering everything up, they made their way back home.

They had just reached the long dirt track up to the house when a car pulled up behind them.

Evie squealed and ran towards the opening door.

'DADDY, DADDY'.

Max bent down and scooped her up in his arms. Touching his nose to hers.

'So what have my two favourite girls been up to today then?'

'We have had a picnic and played ring a roses by the lake. Daddy will you come with us next time?'

'Cross my heart and hope to d………'.

Max fell to his knees. His eyes glazed over. Izzy ran over and grabbed Evie.

'Max? Max what is it?' she saw blood trickling out of his neck where it meets his shoulder.

'Evie I need you to do something for me ok?'

Evie nodded. Albeit she looked terrified, she was also brave.

'Evie I need you to go on home ok and go to your bedroom and lock the door. Don't open it for anyone but me ok. Can you do that for me?'

Again Evie nodded and then ran all the way to the house without looking back.

When Izzy turned round, Max had slumped on to the ground.

'Max, can you hear me. Say something please' she had done her best to stay calm in front of Evie, but now she was beginning to become hysterical.

She shook Max. No response. She leaned down to check he was still breathing. He was. Thank god!

Fuck! Her phone was back at the house. She searched his pockets and found his. She called for an ambulance.

She lifted a hand to her face to wipe the tears away, then screamed when she saw it was covered in blood.

Why was he bleeding? How was he bleeding?

One minute he was just standing there and the next he was on the floor. It didn't make any sense!

Blood. There was blood. The realisation hit her like a ton of bricks………. He had been shot! Someone had shot Max!

But who?

CHAPTER FIFTY-THREE

Izzy had stemmed the blood until the ambulance had arrived.
They had worked fast on Max to stop him losing any more
blood before taking him away.

She had phoned Mrs Hamilton, the housekeeper who lived in
the newly built cottage on the property, to come and stay
with Evie.

Izzy rushed to the hospital, trying to keep within the speed
limit. The last thing she needed was to be pulled over for
speeding.

The police who had arrived literally within five minutes of the
ambulance, were searching the grounds and the outer
perimeter of the land for evidence of the shooter.

When she finally arrived at the hospital, it was in utter chaos.
There had been an traffic accident on the highway and the
hospital staff were rushing about left, right and centre.

She looked for anyone who had a resemblance of someone
who may be the calm within the storm.

Managing to get through the menagerie of people, she
reached the front desk and gave her name and Max's.

The nurse typed in to the computer and nodded.

'Ahh yes. Mr Veto has been taken straight in to theatre. Errm
let me see......' she scrolled down then nodded again 'yes, it's

to remove the bullet that is lodged in his ne…….' she looked up and when she saw the stunned, shocked look on Izzy face, she tried to console her.

'Mrs Veto, once the bullet is removed, it will be plain sailing I'm sure. He will go in to recovery and then you can go and see him. Why don't I get someone to fetch you a cup of sweet tea' the nurse was concerned. She could Izzy was struggling with the noise of the emergency room.

'If you follow me I'll show you in to the family room. It is much quieter in there and I'll go and sort that tea for you'.

Izzy followed and when the nurse left, she slumped down in to one of the armchair. A wave of nausea coming over her, she dropped her head forward between her knees.

Exploring every conceivable possibility as to why Max would have been shot. Her head hurt and she was now getting a migraine.

'Here you are dear, a lovely hot cup of sweet tea' the nurse swept in carrying a tray with the tea and some biscuits too for good measure.

'I just leave it here for you' she placed it down on the coffee table in front of Izzy.

Izzy lifted her head 'Thank you. Is there any news on my husband?' she eagerly asked.

The nurse gave her a sympathetic look 'I haven't heard anything as yet. Why don't I go and see what I can find out for you? Drink your tea. I won't be long'.

It had been half an hour and the nurse hadn't come back. She picked up the now cold cup of tea and took a sip. Pulling a face at the bitter taste, she put the cup back down and stood up. Stretching out her arms she walked over to the door and looked out of the small window. It looked a lot calmer out there. She decided to brave it and opened the door and crashed straight in to a doctor who was entering the room.

'Oh sorry doctor' Izzy said, feeling a little embarrassed.

'Mrs Veto?' He asked.

She nodded. Dread instantly filling her. Was he here to tell me Max is dead? Why else would he be here?

She stumbled forward and the doctor caught her and steadied her.

'Let's go back in here and sit down shall we' he suggested. When they sat down Izzy couldn't look him in the eye. Did she want him to tell her what she already knew? That Max was dead!

'Mrs Veto, as you are aware we had to rush your husband straight in to surgery. The bullet was lodged deep in his neck so it took us a while to remove it as safely as possible. Which we did with success......' he took a deep breath 'We managed to stop the bleeding. We were a little concerned about internal bleeding but we got that under control. However ....'.

OH GOD! HERE IT COMES! She screamed in her head. She lifter here head to the ceiling and closed her eyes. Her breathing becoming deeper and fast as her heart beat raced.

'……. he will make a full recovery. He won't be able to talk properly for a while until he's fully recovered, but he's going to be just fine, Mrs Veto'.

All she could do was squeal with sheer delight. Jumping up and flinging herself at the doctor, almost knocking him off the chair.

CHAPTER FIFTY-FOUR

Max woke up and found Izzy asleep in the comfy chair by his bedside. He looked down and saw her hand on top of his.

He gently lifted her hand off his and held it instead, giving it a soft squeeze.

Izzy opened her eyes and smiled.

'You're awake. Don't ever worry me like that again. You gave us all such a fright. I rang Lorna and she sends her love' she placed a finger on his lips when he tried to speak.

'Rest your voice darling. The doctor said you won't be able to talk for a while until you have recovered.......' She paused.

Max gave her hand a reassuring squeeze.

'The police have been in touch. They found shell casings by the large tree at the top of the ridge. They said it was a sniper gun Max. They said they are following a lead, but I don't know Max. I don't understand who or why anyone would want to shoot you'.

Max pointed to a pad and pencil on the nightstand beside his bed. Izzy handed it to him and watched as he wrote.

When he handed it back to her and she read what he had written. She was stunned to say the least. A bead of sweat started to form above her top lip as she looked at Max and then back at the note pad.

Was he being serious? It couldn't be true, could it? How could it be……. How could it be possible?

He can't be thinking straight. He had been shot and not long since come out of major surgery. Yes, that was it. That's all it was.

With a furrowed brow, she gave Max a puzzled look.

'Darling you must be confused. Your brother is still in prison and will be for a very long time. So you see, it couldn't have been him who shot you' she did her best not to sound condescending.

Max let out a long slow breath, more out of frustration.
Snatching the note pad from her he began writing again……..

I meant Mason must have hired someone

Tell the cops to go interview him

And don't take no for an answer

I love you Izzy

She read it and smiled when she got to the bottom of the page.

'I love you too Max. More than anything. I'll do what you ask. I'll speak to the police and show them what you've wrote, I promise'. She looked at her watch. She had been at the hospital fourteen hours now. She had checked in with the housekeeper a few times to make sure Evie was ok. Mrs Hamilton told her Evie had been asking for her and if daddy was ok.

Izzy had noticed the concern in Mrs Hamilton's voice too so had reassured her as well as Evie that Max was going to be ok.

She leaned over and kissed Max on the cheek.
'I need to go home and check on Evie. I also need a shower and change of clothes. I'm starting to stink' she laughed. Sniffing at herself.

CHAPTER FIFTY-FIVE

Izzy kissed Evie on the cheek. She had laid with her until she had fallen asleep. Trying to explain to a six-year-old that her daddy was ok and would be home soon was tiring to say the least. Especially when you had lacked sleep yourself with worry.

Izzy gently got up from the bed and stopped at the bedroom door, to make sure Evie was still sound asleep before she left the room. Closing the door quietly, Izzy made her way back downstairs and in to the kitchen, where Mrs Hamilton was making them both a cup of tea. She turned around from the sink when she heard Izzy enter the room.

'Is she finally asleep?' Mrs Hamilton said, picking up the teapot and pouring out two cups. She handed one to Izzy.

Izzy sat down at the breakfast table and sighed.

'I hate it when she's upset and hurting. I wish I could wave a magic wand and make everything better'.

'If only' said Mrs Hamilton and smiled.

'I guess I should get something eat. I don't think I have eaten since yesterday'.

'What are you going to do about what Mr Veto asked. You know, about contacting the police about his brother? Are you still thinking of doing it?'

Izzy circled her finger around a tea stain on the table.

'I rang them but they didn't seem that interested to be honest. I think they just humoured me'.

Mrs Hamilton gave her arm a gentle squeeze. The last thing she wanted was sympathy right now.

'Maybe I should just visit Mason and find out for myself' she shrugged. Not really fully committed at her own brainwave and not expecting the reaction she got from Mrs Hamilton.

'Maybe you should dear. If only for your own peace of mind. I could come with you if you like, for moral support'.

Izzy was stunned to say the least. It was only a throw away idea after all. She hadn't meant it, but Mrs Hamilton's response was making the idea sound promising.

'You think it's a good idea then?'

'Oh yes dear. If the police won't do anything, then what else are you supposed to do. Mason won't be expecting you to turn up, so you the element of surprise. He may slip up and tell you everything you need to know'.

She had a point, Izzy thought.

'Ok, let's do it. I'll ring the prison and get a visiting order. Are you sure you want to come with me? Prisons aren't very nice places'.

Mrs Hamilton vigorously nodded. 'Of course, dear, I wouldn't have suggested it otherwise'.

CHAPTER FIFTY-SIX

With Evie, safe at school and armed with Mrs Hamilton by her side, Izzy entered the large electric gates of the prison. To say she was nervous was the statement of the year.

Arm in arm they walked up to the main doors. The guards directed them through the prison and in to the visitors waiting area.

It was grey, cold and dull. The epitome of what a prison should and would look like.

They didn't have wait for very long before their names were called out.

They were shown through to another large room, along with a queue of other people waiting to see their loved ones.

The room contained lots of tables and chairs. No-one was allocated a table and they watched as the other visitors rushed to get the best tables.

'I guess we pick a table' said Izzy.

They chose one closet to where a guard was stood. This way if anything was to kick off, they would feel safe. Be safe.

Izzy leg wouldn't stop bouncing. The nerves had well and truly kicked in and she wondered if she had actually made the biggest mistake of her life coming here.

Mrs Hamilton placed a hand on her knee and gave her a

reassuring smile. She always had a way of making her feel calm only this time she wasn't sure it was working.

'It will be ok Izzy. I'm here and the guard is right there so nothing bad is going to happen. Just ask him your questions and find out what you need to know, then we can get the hell out of this god forsaken hole'.

Izzy chuckled. Yes, it was a god forsaken hole and hopefully she would find out everything in the next ten minutes.

Her only hope was that Mason wouldn't mess her about. But then it was Mason and playing games was what he was good at.

The large door at the other end of the room opened. The prisoners started filing in. Some waved to their loved ones as they crossed the room and some had a sombre look about them.

Izzy waiting in anticipation. Then she saw him. Was it him? He looked different. His hair was longer and tied in to a pony tail and he had a goatee. He looked pretty hot actually. She scolded herself under her breath.

'What was that dear? I didn't hear you' Mrs Hamilton asked. 'Oh nothing. I was just saying that's him' she nodded towards the man now heading for them.

CHAPTER FIFTY-SEVEN

Mason sat down opposite them. He eyed them both with a curiosity that made Izzy suddenly shiver.

He smiled. A smile that would send any woman's legs to jelly. Izzy seemed to be one of them! What the hell was wrong with her?

When he spoke, she was taken aback to hear how gentle his tone was.

'Hello Isabella. Thank you for coming to see me. Unexpected of course but it's nice to see you'. He looked at Mrs Hamilton then.

'I don't believe we've met' he offered his hand.

'Mrs Hamilton. I'm Max and Izzy's housekeeper'. She didn't accept his hand. Mason gave a knowing smile and put his hand down on the table.

'So how have you been? How's Max doing?'

Izzy took a deep breath. 'I'm not here for pleasantries Mason'.

Sighing he leaned back in the chair 'Then why are you here Izzy?'

'I think you know why. I think that everything that has happened these past two weeks is because of ....you' She faulted when she saw the puzzled look on his face.

Could she have been wrong? Could Max have been wrong about his brother being involved in the shooting?

She needed to know for sure.

Mason leaned forward now. He was intrigued. His curiosity now spiked.

'What has happened these last couple of weeks Izzy? Please enlighten me'.

She looked at Mrs Hamilton for encouragement and support and she got it. Mrs Hamilton spoke now.

'Mr Veto, your brother…... Max was shot. The police said it was a sniper……'.

Izzy watched Masons response as Mrs Hamilton explained what had gone on. But his expression never changed. He wasn't giving anything away. This only irked Izzy more than she already was.

She wasn't happy with Mrs Hamilton either as she made the mistake of mentioning Evie!

Izzy looked down at her hands on her lap, as she tried to stifle her anger.

Mason dipped his head to try and catch her eye.

She only looked up when she was stunned by the gentle tone of his voice.

'So you and Max have a daughter' he paused and leaned forward, reaching for her hand.

Without thinking, she lifted her hands and allowed him to embrace them in his.

'I'm so happy for you Isabella. For you and for Max. I'm really glad he found you Izzy and that he's happy at last' he paused again. Squeezing her hands then letting them go.

He sat up straight and took a deep breath.

'I've tried to write to Max so many times over the years, but my guilt stopped me from sending them……. After everything I have done, how could I put my guilt on to him by asking for his forgiveness. Especially when I couldn't forgive myself'.

 'I want to say how sorry I am to you too Izzy. For everything. I'm not asking you to forgive me. I just wanted you to know'. He pushed his chair back and stood up, turning to leave.

'WAIT!! Izzy snapped.

He turned his head but didn't look directly at her.

'It wasn't me Izzy. I didn't ask or arrange for anyone to shoot Max. I'm sorry I haven't got the answers you seek…. good luck to you both. I hope you find whoever did do it'.

CHAPTER FIFTY-EIGHT

Now what? Izzy thought.

Mason could have been lying to cover his ass, even if he did sound sincere!

She gave Mrs Hamilton a sideways glance, as they sped down the highway. She hadn't realised until today just what a speed freak Mrs Hamilton was and made a mental note not to allow Evie to travel in the car with her anymore. Izzy wondered what she thought about what Mason had said though.

'Do you think he was telling us the truth? Mason I mean. Did anything he said sound plausible to you?' Izzy asked.

Mrs Hamilton was looking straight ahead and didn't say anything.

'Mrs Hamilton? Did you hear what I said?'

'Oh yes dear, sorry. I was mulling over what you said.... you know Mr veto better than me dear. Follow your gut is what my mother used to tell me, maybe you should do the same'.

Follow my gut, she said. Just like her mother told her. But her gut was telling her that Mason was telling the truth, which only scared her more because that meant there was someone else out and they wanted Max dead.

Izzy kissed Evie goodnight and crept out of the bedroom and downstairs to find Mrs Hamilton coming out of Max's study.

'Mrs Hamilton, what are you doing in there?'

'Oh errm, nothing really dear. I was just checking to see if it needed cleaning. Dusting and such. I wanted to make sure all is clean and tidy ready for Mr Veto's return'.

Izzy wasn't convinced but let it go. Mrs Hamilton was harmless enough.

'Okay, well I think I'll go and have a long soak then an early night. You may as well get yourself home'.

'What are you going to tell Mr Veto? You are going to the hospital tomorrow? Would you like me to come with you?'

Izzy got a weird feeling in the pit of her stomach. Mrs Hamilton was being overly helpful and it was making her cringe a little.

'No, I'll be fine on my own, but thank you' then as an afterthought 'Why don't you take the next couple of days off. Once Evie is in school I'll be spending my time at the hospital with Max. You've been more than helpful and deserve some time for yourself'.

Mrs Hamilton stared at her. A look of despair that Izzy didn't understand.

'Of course dear, if that's what you think is best' she grabbed her coat and handbag off the chair by the door and without another word, left.

That was weird, thought Izzy. She never would have thought

that Mrs Hamilton could be so disgruntled at something so innocuous.

CHAPTER FIFTY-NINE

Max was sleeping when Izzy entered his room. It had been three weeks now since the shooting and after talking to the doctor just now, he could go home today.

His recovery was remarkable, the doctors had said. They were pleased with how quickly he was healing and happy to discharge him. As long as he rested at home though, their conditions and instructions which Izzy was happy to follow through with.

Max must have heard the door click shut because when she turned he was awake.

'Hey you, how are you feeling?' Izzy said as she walked over and kissed him.

'I actually feel great. The doctor said I can go home tomorrow. I can't wait to see Evie, I've missed her so much……. I have also missed this too….' He pulled her close and kissed her firm on the lips. His hand slowly moving down her back to caress and squeeze her butt.

'Hey, stop that. The doctor said you must rest. I don't think sex is resting much, do you?'

'I feel great Izzy. Stop worrying so much and kiss me. I miss those soft luscious lips of yours' he pulled her close again. Izzy giggled and pulled away.

'You are incorrigible Mr Veto. Now where is your bag. I'll pack your things and once the doctor has signed off, we can get you home'.

Max was resting on the sofa in his study. The open log fire was lit because at dusk the temperature dropped slightly and the doctors had advised that he keep warm.

Izzy was pottering in the kitchen and clock watching.

Mrs Hamilton should have been home with Evie ages ago. Where the hell was she?

Mrs Hamilton had said she would pick Evie up from school so she didn't have to leave Max on his own when they returned from the hospital. Only she seemed to be taking forever.

Maybe she had taken her out for tea instead or for ice-cream or to the park.

Maybe they were dead in a ditch somewhere because Mrs Hamilton was erratic at best, she could have crashed the car!

Oh get a grip Izzy! She scolded herself for being overly dramatic.

She looked at the clock again. It was almost six o'clock.

Izzy paced the kitchen. Should she tell Max? No, she didn't want to wake him while he was resting.

Ring the police? But say what? My housekeeper may or may not have taken my daughter out for tea or possibly crashed the car, but have no idea where? No.

She chewed at her thumb nail, get more and more anxious by

the minute and not having a clue what to do.

Irrationally her only option as far as she could see, was to go and look for them. Where she didn't know, but she had to do something.

She raced through the house to the hall way and snatched up the keys to the 4x4. She was almost out the door when the phone rang, stopping her in her tracks.

CHAPTER SIXTY

Izzy gut feeling was telling her that whoever was on the other end of that phone, was about to give her bad news.

She hesitated. For far too long it seemed, because the phone rang off.

Shit!

She took a step towards the phone. Willing it to ring again.

Max called out from the study.

What did she do? Wait by the phone for it to ring again or see what Max needed?

She chose the latter.

'What is it Max?' she snapped at him impatiently.

'Izzy?' He searched her face. He could see she was restless. Something was bothering her.

'Izzy, tell me what's wrong' he urged.

She was about to speak when the phone rang again. Without hesitation, this time, she ran to the phone in the hall way and snatched up the receiver.

She hadn't realised that of course the phone rang in the study also, so Max had wondered why she hadn't answered that one. So, Max had dragged himself off the sofa and picked up the receiver on his desk.

'Hello'.

'Hello Mrs Veto'.

'Mrs Hamilton? Oh, thank goodness, are you both ok? Is Evie ok? Where are you? I've been so worried but I'm just glad you are both ok. Are you on your way home? Because it's time for Evie's bath......'

'Mrs Veto......' she paused and Izzy heard her take a very loud deep breath. 'Mrs Veto, firstly my name is not Mrs Hamilton......' Izzy cut in 'What you on about? Of course it's you, I recognise your voice anywhere ..i ......'.

'WILL YOU SHUT THE FUCK UP AND LISTEN YOU STUPID WOMAN!' taking another deep breath she began again.

'My name is Margerat Peters. I am the Aunt of Bethany Peters......' she heard Izzy gasp '.....Max's dead fiancé. I took on the persona of Mrs Hamilton to get close to your family. Now I know that it was Mason who murdered her, but I can't get to him can I, so the next best thing is Max'.

Izzy's hand went to her open mouth. This can't be happening. The shock of what she was hearing had made her mute. She had no choice but to listen to continue listening.

'You have a choice Mrs Veto. You either bring me Max or I will kill your daughter. You have two hours to decide. I will call back at eight on the dot.......oh, and Mrs Veto....no cops.....the clock is ticking'. The line went dead.

CHAPTER SIXTY-ONE

Izzy rushed back in to the study. She had to tell Max everything now.

Max was stood by the desk, replacing the receiver. It was then that she realised he must have been listening and heard everything.

'Max! What do we do?'

He stared at her for what seemed like minutes but in reality it was only a couple of seconds.

'We do what she says, that's what. Once you get Evie safe, call the police and tell them everything'.

'Max no! There has to be another way, there just has to be!'

He came across the room and held her tight. Maybe she was right. Maybe there was another way, but time was ticking and he couldn't think of anything else at this moment. This plan was the only thing he had right now.

'There isn't one. Please just do as I ask'.

'But you've just come out of hospital after been shot! You're not strong enough to do anything. Look at you, you can hardly walk! Max please don't do this. Just ring the police, let them deal with it. Please Max I beg of you. Do it for the sake of our daughter'. But her pleading was in vain.

He pushed her away and walked over to the large picture on

the wall behind his desk. Sliding it across, it revealed his safe and punched in the combination.

'That is why I am doing this Izzy, for the sake and safety of our daughter. Did you not hear what she said?' he reached inside the safe and removed a box, placing it down on the desk he opened it. Inside was a gun and bullets.

'What a stupid thing to say, of course I heard what she said! What's that?' she edged her way towards him.

'Holy fuck! Is that a ...a ...a ......'.

'Yes Izzy it's a gun. Now close your mouth and go fetch my coat'.

She did as she was told for once.

'Max, are you absolutely sure about this? I mean, what if she cottons on to what you're doing and hurts Evie?'

'She won't. By the time she realises, you and Evie will be long gone ok. Just leave it to me ok' he grimaced as he attempted to pull his coat on. Izzy helped him.

He gave her a reassuring look and she flung herself at him.

'Max please be safe, I can't lose you now after everything we have already been through. I love you so much'.

'I love you too Izzy and I love Evie and I promise you she will be safe and in your arms before you know it. Now all we have to do is wait for her to ring with instructions'.

Izzy nodded. Then a thought crossed her mind.

'Max'.

'Yes what is it?'

'You heard everything she said didn't you? I mean on the

phone before, about who she really is?'

He slipped the gun in to his coat pocket and looking up at her, he nodded.

'Did you know?'

'Did i know what Izzy?'

'Did you know she was related to your fiancé... to Bethany? Is that why you hired her?'

When he just stared at heard and not answer, she snapped.

'WELL DID YOU!?

'Have you completely lost the leave of your senses. For crying out loud Izzy. No, I didn't know who she was or that she was related to Bethany. In case you forgot she used a different name anyway, so how could I have known....... Now calm down, us arguing isn't helping the situation. Why don't you pour us both a drink while we wait'. He looked at the clock on the mantle. Twenty minutes left. Max sat down on the sofa and laid his head back against the cushion headrest. Poured them both a whiskey. She didn't like it, couldn't even stand the smell but she needed something strong to take away the sting in her heart. The warmth from the liquor would do the job.

She handed Max his drink and sat beside him.

He grabbed her hand and gave it a gentle squeeze.

The phone rang, jolting them out of their temporary calm.

It was only quarter to eight. She was early.

Izzy jumped up and picked up the receiver but Max was too quick and snatched it from her before she could speak.

'YES' he barked.

'Ahh Mr Veto...Max, may I call you Max? You were almost part of the family after all'.

'Call me whatever the hell you want. The important thing is we have a deal. You get me and you let my daughter go. No police just me and Izzy will take Evie to safety. Do we have a deal Mrs Ha.....Margerat whatever the fuck your name is'.

'Yes Max we have a deal. Go to the quarry caves. Be there in thirty minutes' she slammed the phone down.

'What the fuck is it with the quarry and caves that every crank around me has this obsession with!!' it was more a statement than a question.

'Izzy..... IZZY'.

Startled by his abruptness, she whipped her head round to look at him.

'Sorry.... Are you ready to go? Make sure you have your phone. Remember what we planned? The minute you are both safe call the police and tell them where I am. I have my phone too hidden in the lining of my coat, so if she decides to take me on a tour of the countryside, they can trace my phone. Right let's get this show on the road'.

All Izzy could do was nod. She felt numb. She felt scared. Most of all she feared she would never see Max alive again.

CHAPTER SIXTY-TWO

Margerat was standing by the cave entrance with Evie in front of her, holding on to her shoulders when Max and Izzy arrived.

Izzy let out a cry when she saw her daughter. Max steadied her hand on the steering wheel as they pulled to a stop.

'She's ok Izzy. Look she's smiling and waving'.

Izzy looked at Evie. Max was right. She didn't seem distressed or hurt in any way. Small mercies!

They exited the car and began to walk over to the cave.

'Stop right there' Margaret shouted.

They stopped. Izzy began to fidget. If Margerat had hurt a single hair on Evie's head, she would kill her.

'We've had a lovely time haven't we Evie?' Margerat said, looking down at the girl and gently squeezing her shoulders. 'Why don't you tell mummy and daddy what we have done today'.

Evie was excitable now and she rushed her words out to tell them everything they had done.

'Oh mummy, daddy, we've been to the zoo and then had ice-cream and then we came here to explore the caves. They are beautiful too. Can we come another day mummy, daddy?'

Max and Izzy looked at each other, but it was Margerat who

spoke again.

'Hey Max, why don't you come over here and look around the beautiful caves. I'm sure Izzy wants to get Evie home for her bath and ready for bed'.

Izzy grabbed his hand tightly. He squeezed it back in reassurance that everything will be ok.

If only she was as sure.

He turned and kissed Izzy on the cheek and whispered in her ear to do exactly what they had planned.

She nodded and watched him shuffle towards Margerat and Evie.

As he neared Margerat stood to the side to allow him to enter the cave.

'Ok Evie you had better go to your mummy and I'll make sure daddy gets home when he's looked at how beautiful the caves are'.

Evie nodded and said 'Ok Mrs Hamilton. See you tomorrow'.

Hopefully not Izzy thought.

When Evie reached Izzy, she scooped her daughter up in her arms and ran as fast as she could back to the car. Locking the doors, she took out her phone and rang the police, telling them everything.

Now all she had to do was get the hell out of there and hope beyond hope that Max would be ok.

She turned the key in the ignition, but nothing happened. She tried again. Nothing. She tried again and again nothing.

This can't be happening! Not now!

She banged her fists on the steering wheel.

Evie squealed 'mummy what is it?'

She turned around to see Evie crying, looking scared.

'Oh god baby, I am so sorry, I didn't mean to scare you'.

After all what was happening and worrying about Evie, it had been her not Margerat Peters who had made her daughter scared.

She had to think what to do next.

CHAPTER SIXTY-THREE

Thinking on her feet, she felt her only option was to lock Evie in the car and follow Max and Margerat.

From the car, she had seen them leave the cave. Margerat had a gun to Max's back as she made him lead the way.

Izzy knew the police were on their way, so felt safe in the knowledge that Evie would be taken care of and that they would find her, Max and Margerat.

Evie began to panic. She didn't want to be left alone in the car while mummy went to get daddy. She wanted to come too.

'Evie, sweetheart I won't be long. I forgot to tell daddy something and I he doesn't have his phone on him. I promise I won't be long …. Ok?'

Evie scowled.

'Here, take my phone and play on the games. I'll be back before you know it'. She leaned over the seat and kissed her daughter on the forehead.

She exited the car and locked it, then made her way towards the cave.

She popped her head around the corner and saw Max and Margerat heading towards the quarry edge.

She began to follow, dipping behind rocks and shrubs so

Margerat wouldn't see her.

CHAPTER SIXTY-FOUR

Margerat nudged Max towards the quarry edge. Talk about de ja vu!

'Well this is original' Max exclaimed.

'WHAT DO YOU MEAN?' Margerat snapped.

Max then proceeded to tell her about what happened in the exact same spot with Mason.

She studied him for a second, then shook her head.

'Well I won't make that same mistake. Now move'.

Max looked over the edge. His left foot dangerously teetering.

'Move where exactly? There's nowhere else to go'.

'I thought you were more intelligent than that. Where do you think I mean? Over the edge of course. NOW MOVE IT!'

Max's eyes widened in despair. He couldn't believe he was here again. When was all this shit going to end?

He had to try and reason with her at the very least. He rested his arm against his side and felt the hardness of the steel in his pocket. Luckily she hadn't checked him for any weapons. He wondered if he was quick enough though to reach inside his pocket and grab the gun and point it at her, before she realised and shot him with the gun she was already pointing at him.

He had one chance to do it and figured if he could distract her enough, so she would loosen the grip on the gun, he could take control of the situation.

He licked his dry lips moist. He hadn't taken his eyes off her for a second.

'Look, why don't we just talk about this. Try and sort something out. I'm sure neither one of us wanted to be in the position. I know you're blaming me for what happened to Beth, but I did not hurt her. I loved her, I wanted to marry her. My brother …….' He dropped his eyes for a moment as the pain of what happened to Beth shot through his veins and appeared on his face.

'……… It was him that hurt her. He did despicable things to her, and I have had nightmares every night since finding out. You and your family aren't the only ones who have suffered from grief. I have too, even after all these years. Even though I am now married to Izzy and have a child of my own. Having Evie made me understand even more how you feel. If anything happened to Evie, I wouldn't give up until the person responsible was dead.

'But I was not responsible for Beth's death, Margerat and I am so very sorry that I couldn't have stopped it from happening. So please I am begging you now. Please don't leave my wife without a husband and father. Don't make them grieve me like we have all had to do for Beth. Let's just go back to the house and talk and put all this behind us. Let us not stoop to Masons level'.

He could see her thinking. Her eyes darting from left to right as her hand holding the gun faltered slightly.

Now was his chance. He slid his hand slowly in to his pocket and grabbed a hold on the gun.

Still never taking his eyes off her. He gently pulled the gun out of his pocket.

Margerat's hand dropped slightly as she bit her bottom lip. 'Ok, but no poli …..' she looked up at him and stopped speaking when she saw he had a gun pointing at her.

'What the … you lied to me you bastard' she pointed the gun at him, her hand shaking.

'You said we could sort this out. Everything you just said was to fool me, wasn't it? I should have shot you in the cave. By now I would have been too far away for Mrs Veto and the cops to find me. That will teach me not to follow my gut'. Max stepped forward.

'STOP!' she shouted 'DON'T COME ANY CLOSER, OR I WILL SHOOT'. Her eyes scanned around her.

Searching for what Max didn't know but she was obviously becoming more and more agitated.

Margerat was metaphorically backed in to a corner. She could either shoot him or run. She chose the latter, because she didn't think he had it in him to shoot her. He was just protecting himself.

She stepped back slowly. Constantly looking behind her to make sure she didn't trip over anything.

Max took another step forward.

'I SAID STOP. STAY WHERE YOU ARE AND I WONT SHOOT YOU……. I'LL MAKE A DEAL WITH YOU MR VETO…. YOU DON'T SHOOT ME AND I WONT SHOOT YOU, OK?'

Max didn't trust her, but what choice did he have. He had no intentions of shooting her, far from it.

'Ok Mrs Hamil …. I mean Margerat. Go but before you do, throw the gun over in to the quarry. I promise I won't shoot you. I will do the same with mine, but I don't trust you, so you go first'.

The terrified look on her face said it all, but with no other options left, she stepped forward and swinging her arm right back, she threw the gun as far as she could across the quarry. They both stood silent, staring intently at each other as they heard the splash.

'Now it's your turn Mr Vetoooo… HEY GET OFF ME…..ARRGH!'

Margerat fell to the floor as a heavy weight landed on top of her, pinning her to the floor. Blows reigned down on her from balled fists. Someone was screaming at her.

YOU BITCH. YOU NASTY HORRIBLE BITCH. HOW DARE YOU KIDNAP MY DAUGHTER. HOW DARE YOU PUT HER LIFE IN DANGER. BITCH!'

Max had to quickly compose himself from the shock of seeing Izzy rugby tackle Margerat to the floor and who was now punching the crap out of her.

In the distance he heard sirens. The police were almost there. He stumbled across to Izzy and managed to grab hold of her right wrist as she kept pummelling Margerat.

Izzy was far too strong when she was in a rage. He put the gun back in his coat pocket and tried to grab her other wrist. But the pain from his gun shot would made him grimaced and cry out in pain. It was this that stopped Izzy in her tracks. She looked up at Max and seeing his pain, she climbed off the top of Margerat and into Max's arms.

It was at this moment the police arrived and taking in the scene, they cuffed Margerat and took her away.

Izzy was sobbing against Max's chest as he comforted her. 'Hey. It's ok now. It's over. We're ok'. He bent his head and tilting her chin up, he kissed her softly.

Behind them they heard an excited squeal. It was Evie. A female officer had escorted her to them.

'Mummy, daddy there you are. Why are the police here? Why is Mrs Hamilton with them?'

'Evie, sweetheart. Come here and give me a cuddle. You sure are a sight for sore eyes' Max bent down and opened his arms to embrace her.

'Daddy what's happening? Is there something wrong?'

'No darling, everything is fantastic, isn't it mummy' he looked over at Izzy who smiled and nodded.

'Yes Evie. Everything is fantastic now'.

ACKNOWLEDGEMENTS

I would like to give a big thank you to my husband Darran, for is unconditional love and support. You are my rock and my muse.

To my son, Cameron and his fiancé Georgina for their encouragement and support.

To my son Lewis for his continued love and support of my endeavours.
To my friend Karen. You give me the much-needed kick up the butt. I would be slobbing on the sofa otherwise, still dreaming about writing.

To my Pa (step-dad) for just being the lovable miserable cantankerous old grump that you are.

To everyone else who has supported and encouraged me.

I love you all very much.

Thank you.

Printed in Great Britain
by Amazon